Even More Tales
Most Strange

Jeremy Hayes

For Noosh, Ash, and Loki, my support at home.

Other Books By Jeremy Hayes

The Stonewood Trilogy

Book I: The Thieves of Stonewood

Book II: The Demon of Stonewood

Book III: The King of Stonewood

Tales Most Strange

The Goblin Squad

Evonne and Vrawg: Bounty Hunters

Northlord Publishing

Visit us at: www.northlordpublishing.com for news about upcoming releases or to contact the author.

Website/Logo: Cody Kotsopoulos www.kotsysdesigns.com

CONTENTS

INTRODUCTION

Here we are with another collection of tales that are most strange. I had so much fun writing the first collection, and since there was considerable interest in the first book, especially from the wonderful folk in the UK, I decided another collection was in order. Much like the first Tales Most Strange, you will find a wide variety of different stories, featuring witches, wizards, fortune tellers, and even the return of Detective Edward Kane.

I was quite pleased to have a story of mine accepted and printed in Weirdbook Magazine. After the disappearance of the famous Weird Tales Magazine, some of those involved revived Weirdbook after a twenty-year hiatus. My story Vandegald's Globes was first printed in issue number 36 of Weirdbook, which was published in August 2017. I have included that story in this collection. I have also had many of the stories from my last book reprinted by Rainfall Books in the UK, who publish wonderfully-weird chapbooks with really fantastic covers. It's all been very exciting.

Needless to say, I am happy that people are enjoying my stories all over the world and I will keep writing them for as long as the weird ideas keep coming. Enjoy!

- Jeremy Hayes

VANDEGALD'S GLOBES

The chimes above the shop's door played their soft melody to announce the arrival of another potential customer. The middle-aged man behind the counter looked up from a dusty tome and straightened his black robe.

The customer was female and fairly attractive, with her auburn hair tied up into a bun. It was a simple enough task to deduce that she was well off. Perhaps not the status of a Lady, and yet still upper-class. Her clothes were obviously expensive and she walked with an air of nobility; of someone who was used to getting what she wanted.

The woman browsed through a few of the shop's knick-knacks before the man behind the counter spoke.

"Excuse me, my dear, is there anything that I may help you with?"

The woman looked up with a start, not having noticed that there had been someone watching her. The shop was so cluttered with various items that the man behind the counter had just blended in with the scenery. He had a neatly-trimmed salt-and-pepper beard to match his hair of the same color. After seeing nearly fifty-three years, his hair was now more salt than pepper.

He wore a simple, nondescript black robe and several silver rings were visible on both of his hands. His smile was a friendly one and his eyes bespoke of a calm, gentle, demeanor.

"I am sorry, I did not notice you standing there."

"I apologize for giving you a start. I am Vandegald, the owner of this den of antiquities. Is there anything you were looking for in particular?"

"Nothing specific, no. My nephew's birthday is approaching and I just wanted to get him something more unique."

"How old is your nephew, if I may inquire?"

"He is turning ten."

"And his interests? Knights, perhaps? Gladiators?"

"Monsters," the woman blushed.

"Ah, not so strange for a lad of ten," Vandegald smiled. "I can recall my own interests in the creatures that prowled through the shadows of my room and hid out of sight beneath my bed."

"Yes, you boys."

"We are guilty of silly interests. And I am afraid we carry those on into our twilight years, as well."

"So, do you have anything monster related at all? Perhaps a carving, or even a painting? Nothing too gruesome, mind you, I don't want to be the one responsible for giving him nightmares."

"Indeed, I do have a few such things laying about.

Though, depending on your budget of course, I have something that he may find of particular interest."

"Oh?"

"Yes, please step this way, I keep them on the shelf here behind the counter. They are quite fragile so I prefer to keep them out of reach."

The woman approached the counter and watched the man pull down three objects from the shelf, very carefully, and one at a time. He sat them on the counter in front of her for inspection.

"How lovely. What are they exactly?"

"I call them Vandegald's Globes."

The items were indeed glass globes, resting on ornately-carved wooden bases. They almost appeared similar to a wizard's crystal ball, only the globes were not empty. Each globe consisted of a different scene. The first one held the ruins of a tiny castle, the second had a mountain with a dark cave at the base, and the third housed a tiny cabin, surrounded by a swamp.

"Good heavens, what is that?" the woman said, jumping back.

She had spotted movement from the second globe, with the cave. From within the cave, emerged a tiny bat-like creature. It hovered in front of the cave entrance with black wings and looked up at the woman with sickly-yellow eyes."

"That is a bolgrock, or I should say, the illusion of a bolgrock."

"A bolgrock?"

"Yes. A bolgrock is a type of minor demon that roams the Abyss. As you can see it would have a certain appeal to a child of ten."

"I find it hideous, but yes, I see what you mean. It isn't real, you say?"

"No, no, of course not. A bolgrock is nothing you want to toy with, I assure you. You see, I studied magic in the City of Seven Towers for a time. I studied illusion, to be exact. I have cast a spell of illusion on the globes. Each globe consists of a different creature and that creature will move about from time to time and behave as if it is very much alive. Sometimes the bolgrock will hide within the mountain cave, and other times, like now, it will fly about the globe."

"Why, that is brilliant. What is in the other two globes?"

"The globe with the castle contains the illusion of a ghost. When there is little to no light in the room, the ghost will appear from within the castle and roam about. And the third, well there you go, the third contains a troll as you can see now."

The woman's eyes widened as she watched a miniature troll shuffle through the scenery of a swamp.

"I must know how much these cost."

"I am afraid they are not very budget-friendly, but I assure you they are unique. You will find nothing quite like them anywhere in Zalhandria or Tauros. Or the rest of the world, I might add."

"So, how much?"

"Well, I sell them for one hundred gold pieces each. The bases are all hand-carved by me, as well. Much work goes into the construction of just one globe. But seeing as how I can always use some word-of-mouth advertising, and seeing as how it is your nephew's birthday, I would be willing to sell you one for fifty."

"Fifty gold is a lot more than I was expecting to spend on my nephew but that is a good deal you have offered me. I am sure this could guarantee that I become his favorite aunt."

"Of that I have no doubt."

"Does your offer apply to two of them? My brother is always reading tales of ghosts and I am sure he would enjoy your ghost globe."

"Absolutely. Two globes for one hundred gold pieces, today only. I would appreciate if you not tell any others of the deal I have given you. The price goes back to one hundred each once you exit my shop."

"Understood, and I thank you."

"So, the ghost for your brother, and have you decided which one your nephew may like the most?"

"Hmm, I do know he is fascinated by trolls but that, bolgrock, you said? Yes, the bolgrock is positively frightening. I think I will take that one."

"A fine choice, my dear. Your nephew will be delighted, I can guarantee it. Allow me to package them up carefully for a safe journey home."

"Much appreciated."

Vandegald wrapped each globe individually with paper and placed each within its own box. He made sure it was a snug fit to prevent them from being jostled about. The woman counted out one hundred gold pieces, a large amount for one person to be carrying around at any one time, and thanked the man for his generous deal.

Once she had exited the shop, Vandegald took the gold into a back room and stored it away inside of a safe he had hidden under a floorboard. The man smiled. That made six globes sold just this week. He did not mind selling the last two at a discounted price. It meant that one of them was going to be showcased at a birthday party. He was confident that when others got a peek at one of his globes, there would be more people wishing to purchase one for themselves. His troll globe was the last one left in stock, which meant he had better get started on crafting several more. He would need to start tonight.

The afternoon passed slowly, with only a few minor sales the rest of the day. Night descended on the city of Moorstead and Vandegald closed his shop. He found that very few decent folk roamed the streets at night. The night belonged to vagrants and undesirable types. Three different locks were used to secure his front door from curious thieves.

Vandegald lived within his shop. He had a small apartment located directly above the shop and a basement below, where he did his work. After filling his belly with some leftover stew, he retired to the basement for the rest of the evening.

The narrow winding stairs to his basement workshop creaked noisily as Vandegald descended. He had always mused that no burglar could catch him unaware down there. Not even a master thief could navigate those stairs silently, he figured.

The workshop was devoid of any windows and was cast in complete darkness. Vandegald utilized a small lantern in order to move about and light some candles. The candles managed to chase away much of the shadows and provided enough light to read by.

Fortunately, he had several carved bases already finished, along with a few globes that contained their scenery. Now all they required were their occupants. The bolgrock was one of his more popular globes so he decided to craft one of those ones first.

Vandegald Skaldanos was a sorcerer of no small measure. While it was true that he spent most of his life studying magic in the City of Seven Towers, it was not actually the art of illusion that he studied. Vandegald's main interest was in odd creatures, and more specifically, creatures from other worlds and planes of existence. He was most fascinated by those creatures that made the Abyss their home; all varieties of demons and devils. The bolgrock, of course, was one of those creatures. Bolgrocks were considered a demon of lesser-note but Vandegald found them fascinating all the same.

The City of Seven Towers, located in the southern nation of Zalhandria, was a haven for wizards and sorcerers of all levels of expertise. The city itself was ruled by seven wizards who occupied the seven towers. Vandegald had studied under Torglad the Mad, a great summoner who was rumored to have gone mad from his many dealings with denizens of the Abyss.

With sorcerers being a silver coin a dozen in that city, Vandegald had decided to leave when he felt he had learned all that he could from Torglad. He sought out a city where he and his magical skills would be seen as more unique. The sorcerer settled in the city of Moorstead, which sat in the northern reaches of Zalhandria, just beyond the Zal-Baron Desert and bordering with the lands of Tauros.

Vandegald was also a collector of strange items from all corners of the world and had opened a shop to deal in such things. It was only within the last year, that he begun crafting his globes and making them available for sale. So

far they had been selling well with the residents of
Moorstead and with travelers and merchants who were
only passing through.

Vandegald opened an old tome that rested on his
workshop table and turned the yellowed-pages to the
appropriate spot. He paced around the room, inspecting
the circle he had painted on the floor, to be absolutely sure
that it was perfect. He also ensured that every candle and
every painted rune outside the circle was in their proper
place. It was crucial that everything be exact. One small
mistake could prove disastrous.

Once everything seemed to be in order, Vandegald
retraced his steps and checked everything over a second
time. Many were the tales of wizards, who in haste, and
lacking patience, had rushed into a spell that brought
doom upon them. Vandegald never wanted to star in his
own tale of a foolish wizard. He had always been
meticulous in his work.

Nodding in satisfaction, he picked up the tome and
began reading a spell aloud. Torglad the Mad had this
particular spell committed to memory. It was a fairly
complex spell, written in an unused language, so
Vandegald always felt more comfortable reading from the
book.

Beads of sweat formed on his forehead as his voice
rose, nearing the end of the spell. He closed his eyes and
then spoke the final word, slamming the book shut. A
blast of hot air buffeted his face, messing his hair, slightly.

When his eyes opened, he was greeted with a familiar
sight. Inside his summoning circle hovered a bolgrock.
The black-skinned creature of the Abyss was held aloft by
its bat-like wings. The three-foot tall demon cast him a

hateful stare with its sickly-yellow eyes. It glanced about, immediately recognizing that it was trapped within the wizard's magical circle.

The bolgrock let out a skin-shivering screech, and then moments later, was sucked into the nearest globe. Vandegald walked over to regard his newest creation. The bolgrock flew about in a frenzy, looking for any way out of its tiny prison, but of course, there was none.

Each globe was painstakingly warded with protective spells prior to the summoning. The globe was able to suck in its occupant but nothing could leave. Inside the globe, time seemed to stand still, or at very least, slow down, quite considerably. The globe's occupant could survive without food and water for an indefinite amount of time. Torglad had perfected this spell in order to imprison demons and devils for study. He wished to keep them alive for great lengths of time, without having to feed or hydrate them. Vandegald was unsure of just how long the globe's occupant could survive but he had yet to witness one perish.

The sorcerer smiled; he was pleased with his work. Casting the spell was taxing, so Vandegald gave himself a break before summoning a second bolgrock and making another globe. He retired to his bed for the night, after also summoning a troll from the Whisper Marsh. Three globes in one evening was a fine accomplishment.

The next few weeks flew by and business was good. Vandegald was averaging one globe sold per day and some days he sold two. Each evening was spent carving new bases, enchanting globes, and then summoning the appropriate creature. Bolgrocks and trolls continued to be a customer favorite and some folk were beginning to make requests.

"Can you make one with an ogre?"

"How about a wraith?"

"I would like one with a dragon," they said.

Summoning different types of creatures was no simple task. One had to know of a location to summon them from. Vandegald had studied a variety of books on the Abyss which made summoning the bolgrocks much easier. He had made several excursions into the Whisper Marsh where many trolls made their home. He gathered ghosts from the Pallantyr Valley, the site of an ancient battleground where tens of thousands of warriors lost their lives.

The sorcerer knew of only one location, where dwelt a dragon, but he dared not attempt that summoning. He was not even sure if it was possible, and even if it were, he would not risk it.

One quiet afternoon, a potential customer made a most curious request. His young son was fascinated by gladiators and offered to buy a globe that featured one. Vandegald informed the man that he did not have such a globe and that the illusion required to create a gladiator was not a simple one. The man was quite wealthy and offered three times the normal amount if Vandegald could craft one for his son. The sorcerer lay awake all night, pondering that request.

The following day, Vandegald paid a visit to the city of Gladenfar. Gladenfar was a port city along the southern coast of Zalhandria and was famous for its gladiatorial arena. Travel to that city by normal means could have taken a month but Vandegald had a spell that made it instantaneous. He opened a magical gate in his basement and when he stepped through, he was instantly transported outside the walls of Gladenfar.

He was granted entry into a holding area which housed many gladiators. Gladenfar's gladiators were all slaves and Vandegald posed as a potential buyer. When the timing was just right, and no prying eyes were about, the sorcerer cast the necessary spell that sucked one of the poor warriors into the globe that he had brought with him. Vandegald was back in Moorstead before the man was ever missed.

The globe featured an arena scene, and much like any of the imprisoned creatures, the gladiator explored his new prison, seeking a way out of his living nightmare. Vandegald made sure the man was unarmed so he would be unable to take his own life if madness took him.

It was the first time that he had crafted a globe using a human and he had mixed emotions about it. There was a moral line that he had never crossed before; only using savage creatures for his creations. Though, the three hundred gold pieces helped quiet his conscience. The customer was pleased and his son was ecstatic. So, Vandegald continued on with little regard for the trapped gladiator.

A month later, another request was brought to his attention. This customer, much like Vandegald himself, was well-versed in the creatures of the Abyss. He was a wealthy lord who studied demonology.

"A ghastly hobby, some people say, but I collect all things Abyssal," Lord Ryerdon stated. "Tomes, statues, weaponry. Any relic, really, that relates to the Abyss."

"I can quite understand your interest, really I do," Vandegald replied. "I have read a book or two and developed more than just a mild fascination."

"Ah, a brother-in-demon-arms."

"Quite. So what can I do for you?"

"Well, I have seen your globes. Fantastic creations, if I may say."

"Thank you."

"I would love to purchase one to display with the rest of my collection."

Vandegald lifted one of the globes from the shelf behind the counter and placed it in front of Lord Ryerdon. "This bolgrock might interest you, then."

"Hmm, well, as interesting a creature as the bolgrock is, I know of several other people who own a globe just like it. I was hoping for a globe a little more unique. Perhaps a globe better suited to my tastes."

"I am afraid as far as denizens of the Abyss go, the bolgrock is the only globe I have available."

"Is crafting the illusion of another creature really that difficult? Pardon my ignorance, I know nothing of magic and its workings."

"Without going into the boring details, it certainly can be, yes. I have perfected the illusion of the bolgrock. Creating a different creature for the globe is a longer and more difficult process."

"I will gladly pay."

"It is not just a matter of…"

"How about one thousand gold pieces?"

"One thousand?"

"Yes, one thousand. But I want it unique. I want a four-armed zairgoth, or a xano-fiend, or even a devil."

Vandegald paused to consider whether he could even pull it off and Lord Ryerdon took his silence as a reluctance to accept the gold he offered.

"Two thousand, then. I want a one-of-a-kind demonic globe that nobody else possesses. It will become an honored piece in my collection."

The sorcerer rubbed his chin and nodded. "I will certainly give it my best effort."

Lord Ryerdon placed a piece of paper onto the counter. "Splendid. This is my address. Have a message sent to me when it is complete. But please do not make me wait too long, I beg."

Vandegald nodded again and Lord Ryerdon took his leave. The sorcerer sat down in his chair behind the counter to ponder his situation. Two thousand gold pieces was far too large an amount to pass up, but could he do it? He knew it was possible. He had witnessed Torglad summon several greater demons and even the odd devil. But to summon those, he required the creature's name.

In the world of sorcerers, names brought power. Vandegald knew he had recorded the names of a few demons and devils in one of his own notebooks, before he left the City of Seven Towers. He also possessed tomes which named a few others. Summoning those types of creatures, devils especially, who ruled over the Abyss, was something that could not be taken lightly. Vandegald did believe he was capable, though. He would need to strengthen the wards surrounding his summoning circle and prepare a few other defenses, in the event that something unforeseen arose, but he felt he could do it.

Vandegald's shop was open for business but he spent much of the next day behind the counter, pouring over numerous books. Customers came and went and he paid them little heed. His mind was consumed with the task ahead. He searched his library, desperately, seeking a name to use for the summoning. He decided against using any of the names he had recorded in his own notes. Those names were taken from Torglad and Vandegald had no idea whether any of those creatures were still in existence. Also, if he had made any mistake in recording the name correctly, the consequences could prove horrendous.

Late into the night, before retiring to bed, Vandegald smiled; he had found what he was looking for. The old tome was titled, Valysha's Guide to the Abyss. Valysha was apparently a sorceress of immense power who had traveled to the Abyss on many occasions, recording her experiences, and most importantly, the names of those she had encountered. Satisfied with his find, Vandegald planned to read further in the morning and turned in for the night.

As the following morning became afternoon, Vandegald had a name. Xalboda Vaxalian, a devil of considerable power and influence, and a prince among devils. Not only did the book provide Xalboda's full name, but detailed his castle and its location within the Abyss. Vandegald felt he had everything he required to summon and trap this particular devil. He believed he would be ready to attempt the summoning in two days' time.

"Ah, excuse me, I hate to interrupt," a voice suddenly said.

Vandegald looked up from his seat behind the counter to find three gentlemen standing in his shop. How long they had been there, only they knew.

"Sorry, I was little preoccupied with my reading," the sorcerer said, standing up.

The tall man in the middle was very well-dressed, a

lord no doubt. The two men flanking him wore chain mail vests with swords hanging by their sides; bodyguards most likely.

"How may I help you gentlemen?" Vandegald inquired.

"You must be Vandegald?"

"I am."

"It is a pleasure to meet you. I am Lord Stainford. It would seem your globes are the talk of the town. I am quite impressed with your work."

"Thank you, you flatter me."

"My daughter is even more impressed, than I. In fact, your globes are all she can talk about, as of late. I am here to place an order as a gift for her."

"I have several on the shelf here behind me."

"I have seen most of your work so far. However, my daughter has very little interest in monsters. By chance, do you have any other types of globes? Something less frightening for a young girl?"

"I am afraid I do not. Not currently. I would have to craft a new globe, just for her. It would be slightly more expensive."

"I am sure we can come to an arrangement. This would mean a lot to me and to her, if you could do that."

"I could do it for two hundred gold pieces."

"That sounds reasonable to me."

"Excellent. Give me two days, Lord Stainford, and I will have a globe here for your daughter."

"Thank you, Vandegald. We shall return in two days."

When Vandegald was alone again, he figured crafting a globe for the man's daughter would be simple enough. If she wasn't interested in monsters, he would find her a bunny, or perhaps a fox. He thought he may even be able to acquire a fairy.

The sorcerer cast aside all thoughts of the young girl's globe and dove back into Valysha's book, concentrating fully on the more difficult task in front of him. He closed his shop early that day and went straight to the basement to make the necessary preparations. On the following day, when he was absolutely positive that everything was ready, he decided it was time for the summoning.

Vandegald's hands trembled slightly as he held the spellbook in front of him. He took a few deep breaths and then began the casting. This spell was more involved and took longer than usual. The casting ended as Vandegald shouted the name, Xalboda Vaxalian. For a few brief moments, the candles in the room were extinguished, leaving the sorcerer standing in pitch-darkness. When they flared back to life, Vandegald gasped, his jaw hanging open in surprise.

Standing in the center of his summoning circle was not the devil-prince he was expecting, but a stunningly-attractive human woman. The raven-haired beauty immediately looked about at her surroundings, wearing a look of surprise that was equal to Vandegald's. Her eyes went wide when she noticed the sorcerer.

"Am I free? Have you really rescued me from the vile clutches of Xalboda? I cannot thank…"

The woman's sentence was cut short and replaced with an ear-splitting scream as her body was sucked into the globe that Vandegald had prepared. Vandegald was speechless and watched in horror as the innocent woman now stood next to a castle of red brick within her tiny glass prison. She fell to her knees and wept, not understanding what had just happened to her.

A million thoughts ran through Vandegald's mind. How had his spell gone awry? Apparently he had summoned a prisoner from within Xalboda's castle and not Xalboda himself. And it was a woman, a human woman of exceptional beauty. Vandegald could not leave this woman inside the globe and immediately set to work on dispelling the protective wards around it.

With the wards eliminated, the sorcerer did the only thing that he could; he teleported inside the globe. He planned to grab the woman and teleport them both back outside. Once inside his own globe, Vandegald took a moment to look around and finally get the view of the world that all the other occupants of his globes shared. Everything outside of the globe appeared giant-sized, and slightly distorted, due to the shape of the glass.

"Who are you?" the woman said, standing and wiping tears from her beautiful green eyes.

"I am Vandegald and I have apparently made a huge mistake. Take my hand and I will get us out of here."

The woman accepted Vandegald's extended hand and the sorcerer was surprised by how warm her skin felt against his. It sent a soothing feeling up his arm and spread throughout his body. She leaned in to kiss her would-be rescuer and Vandegald was helpless to resist. His lips tingled and went numb when she placed hers against his. She kissed Vandegald deeply and his knees went weak. The sorcerer slowly slumped to the ground, feeling completely paralyzed. He was unable to move or even to speak.

The woman smiled wickedly as her pale skin turned a shade of red. Two small horns sprouted from her forehead and black, leathery wings, unfolded from behind her back.

She spoke a few words in a demonic language and vanished. Only Vandegald's eyes could move and he shifted his gaze upwards, noticing that the strange woman was now outside the globe, looking in.

Possessing an extensive knowledge of magic, the woman picked up one of Vandegald's spellbooks and renewed the protective wards onto the globe. The effects of her paralyzing kiss soon wore off and Vandegald got to his feet, staring up at her. He attempted his spell of teleportation, but of course, it had failed. The demonic-woman laughed.

She picked up Valysha's Guide to the Abyss and held it toward the globe. "I see you have read my book," she laughed again. "There is no Castle Bloodborn and there is no devil-prince that dwells there. I am Xalboda Vaxalian, a succubus. I wrote that book and saw to it that it reached the land of mortals. I wanted fools like you to summon me and fall prey to my charms. Thank you for freeing me from the Abyss, Vandegald. And know that your name is well-known among us. Did you think that your summonings would go unnoticed by the powers of the Abyss? It was only a matter of time before one of us got you. I am pleased that it was me. Now, how will you like living in your tiny little prison, I wonder?"

Xalboda picked up the globe and made her way into Vandegald's shop. A knock at the door surprised her and she placed the globe on the counter. By the time she unlocked the door, she resembled a human female once more.

A young man wore a shocked expression at the sight of the woman in Vandegald's shop. "H-hello, g-good afternoon, my lady. Is Vandegald about?"

"Oh he is about, but is unable to receive company. I, on the other hand, am free," she purred.

"Excuse m-me?"

"I am new here and would like a tour of your city. Would you be so kind as to show me around?"

The young man found the woman's request irresistible and nodded, foolishly, like a young school-boy. The succubus smiled widely and took the man's arm in hers, strolling from the shop.

*   *   *   *

"Hello? Hello? Vandegald? Are you here?" Lord Stainford called.

The wealthy lord had returned to the shop with one of his men-at-arms. They found the door unlocked, though Vandegald was nowhere in sight. The pair had waited, impatiently, until they decided to take a look around.

Lord Stainford stuck his head into the back room. "Vandegald? Vandegald, are you there? I have returned for my daughter's globe."

"My lord, this must be it here on the counter," the other man said.

Lord Stainford joined him at the counter.

"See here, there is a packing box with your name on it. Something must have distracted Vandegald and he never got around to it. This globe must be yours."

"Hmm, you must be correct. I wonder what he has created for me."

Lord Stainford peered into the globe, admiring the craftsmanship of the tiny red castle. He tapped on the glass of the globe and then lifted and shook it when no illusion had first appeared.

"My goodness, how exquisite."

The wealthy lord marveled at the sight of a miniature Vandegald, exiting the little castle. The illusion of the wizard jumped up and down, waving his arms in the air, almost as if it was actually aware of the two men looking down upon it.

"Magnificent. Look at the detail. It's a spitting image of the man himself. Oh, Vandegald, you old rascal, you have truly outdone yourself this time. My daughter will love it. Vernon, leave the payment behind the counter some place where Vandegald will find it when he returns. I can't wait to get home and give Nella her gift."

THE POSSESSED

It was always hot here but today was unusually hot. The sky was a deep red and I knew I had my work cut out for me this time. We approached the ancient keep and there was a hesitance to my step. Not because I was afraid, no, but because I had a reputation to uphold. The information I was given by the temple told me this case would be a difficult one.

I paused at the front gate and turned to my coworker. "Perhaps, you should wait out here. This may get a little rough."

"Are you positive? I can help."

"No, trust me, you will be safer out here. I must do this one alone."

He reluctantly nodded and I proceeded through the gate, which had been left open in anticipation of my arrival. I knew my longtime friend wished to help but I truly felt that this time he may only get in the way. I did not wish to worry for his safety as well. I knew the risks and I was better prepared for all outcomes. He was still young and inexperienced. This one I would have to do alone.

I ascended the stone steps to a set of iron-bound double doors. I reached for the door knocker but the entrance way opened. A servant nodded and indicated for me to follow. There was no need for introductions. He knew who I was and time was of the essence.

The servant held a candle to light our way through the dark corridor. We passed several lavishly-furnished rooms but I had no time to admire the décor. My mind was set on the task ahead of me.

My escort unlatched a thick door and led me down a narrow winding staircase. I assumed we would have been heading upwards toward the living quarters in the keep's tower. The fact that we were now heading down into the dungeons told me this was serious indeed.

It was an unpleasant thought that the daughter of a powerful lord had to be humiliated and locked in a dark dungeon. I felt for the family. This was a difficult time for them. The lord of the keep held much influence in this region and if word got out about his daughter's condition, it could prove damaging. Discretion was paramount. My lips were sealed about such cases and I felt it was nobody else's business anyhow. Once I was called in to deal with a situation, I knew the family had exhausted all other resources and were now at their wits' end. I would do everything within my power to remedy this as quickly and as quietly as possible.

A few twists and turns brought us into a dank chamber that was illuminated by four torches; one per wall. The room was devoid of furnishings, save for one table that sat in the center. The poor unfortunate lord's daughter lay on the table, chained down by her wrists and ankles. Her parents stood close by; weeks' worth of worry was etched upon their faces. This had taken a toll on them. They appeared to have aged over this ordeal.

The lord's face did brighten, somewhat, as he turned to regard my arrival. He came toward me and meant to speak, but I held a finger to my lips and indicated he remain silent. There would be time for pleasantries later, I had hoped. Now was not the time.

The servant bowed and exited the room. I made a gesture with my hand, suggesting that the others follow him but they shook their heads. They were determined to see this through. While I thought it best that they leave, I could not argue with a parent's desire to remain by their daughter's side in such a time as this. I would have probably done the same, despite the perils that were present.

I placed my bag onto the smooth stone floor and decided to inspect the lord's daughter before beginning anything further. So far, I only had second-hand information that was given to me about her condition. I needed to determine how grave this was for myself.

Her eyes were closed but her limbs were in constant motion, fighting against the iron restraints that kept her immobile on the table. The lord was wise to restrain her as such, to prevent her from harming herself, and most definitely others. A necessary precaution with these extreme cases.

Her skin color appeared off. It was paler than it should have been and it seemed as though she had lost much weight. Her once pretty face now looked gaunt, with protruding cheek bones.

I placed a hand on her forehead and it felt chilled. Not a good sign at all. The lord may have waited too long in sending for my help but I truly hoped that was not the case.

I attempted to lift an eyelid with my thumb, when both her eyes shot open and she snarled, causing me to jump back with a start. Her pupils had vanished behind a silvery glow. I silently whispered a prayer to a specific god. This was worse than I had originally thought. The monster inside her had already taken a firm hold.

I composed myself quickly, not wishing to overly alarm the lord and his wife. It was time I began.

"Amelaxia," I said, using her name. "I am here to free you of this monster. I know you are still in there, somewhere. I need you to be strong and hang in there. Only together, with our strength combined, will we prevail here."

She snarled again and spat at me, threatening to break free of her restraints. For a moment, I worried, but they seemed to be strongly-built and held her in place. She was small but the beast inside her provided supernatural strength. Were she to get free, it would create a world of problems for us all.

I pulled out a carved symbol from my bag and held it over her. I began chanting in an ancient language that was seldom used. Very few even knew of its existence, as it was from a time long forgotten. Each syllable caused Amelaxia to thrash about. She growled; her eyes glowing brightly with a silver radiance.

"The spirit that resides inside the body of Amelaxia is

not welcome!" I shouted. "You must leave her! You must leave this world entirely and never return! Do you hear me?"

"She is mine now," she spoke, but the voice was not her own. It was a soft melodic voice that caused my skin to crawl. "Her soul is mine and you cannot have it back."

I chanted louder and began circling the table. The lord and his wife clung to each other tightly; their faces were masks of horror. Amelaxia howled in distress.

I took a black-bladed dagger from my bag and sliced into my thumb. As it began to bleed, I pressed my thumb onto her forehead and drew a symbol. Her body immediately convulsed with pain.

"You unholy priest!" she screamed. "You cannot have her back!"

The lord shouted a warning as her right hand broke free. The iron shackle around her wrist shattered and she reached for me. Fortunately, I proved the quicker and pulled back in time. She ripped a strip off my black robe but that was all. I nodded a silent thanks to the lord.

I crouched down and searched my bag for a particular vial. It contained water that I had cursed just before leaving my home. I pulled out the cork and downed a mouthful of the liquid before handing it toward the lord and his wife.

"Take a sip, each of you. When that monster leaves her body it will seek another to inhabit. This will prevent it from entering ours."

With trembling hands, the lord's wife drank first. After the lord had also taken a sip, he handed the vial back to me. I quickly grabbed Amelaxia by the jaw and forced the rest of the liquid down her throat, being mindful of her right hand which was looking to claw at my skin.

The girl vomited a black acidic substance that burned small holes into my robe. The table smoked where drops of the vomit had landed. It was time for the final stage.

"Please, my Lord, some assistance."

"What do you need?" he asked, with a quiver in his voice.

"Grab her arm and hold it down, while I draw the last symbol. Careful, now, do not let her grab you."

The lord was imbued with great strength and did as instructed. He grabbed his daughter's wrist and held her arm down, though, it took all of his immense strength to do so. His arms shook and he gritted his teeth, growling.

I tore Amelaxia's nightshirt and used my thumb to draw the final symbol with my own blood, directly above her heart. She screamed and trashed and spat but I finished the symbol and chanted the last words, loudly.

As the last syllable left my lips, a great wind roared through the chamber and extinguished the torches. The room would have been cast into total darkness if it were not for Amelaxia's glowing silver eyes. Her back arched and she squealed with an otherworldly shriek.

Amelaxia vomited again, only this time, a golden mist shot forth from her mouth. It sparkled with a radiance so bright that it stung our eyes to behold it. The mist took on a humanoid shape with two large wings. It floated around the room, seeking a new host, but found no vessel with which to inhabit. The cursed water had done its duty.

A mouth formed on its misty face and it opened in a silent sigh of disappointment. Then it was gone.

"Quickly, the torches," I said in the pitch darkness that followed the monster's departure.

I heard the lord fumbling around until the first torch flared back to life and allowed us to assess the situation. Amelaxia laid on the table, panting quickly with exhaustion. Her eyes were closed and she had ceased her attempts to break free of the remaining shackles. Her right arm rested limply by her side.

The three of us rushed to the table and Amelaxia suddenly sensed our presence.

"Mother? Father?" she said weakly, in her own voice.

Her eyes fluttered open and her previous silver orbs were now blood red. I let out a giant sigh of relief. She was saved.

The mighty demon lord turned to me and placed a strong hand on my shoulder. "I do not know how to thank you, Xoraxelstein. I was told you were the best exorcist in all the Abyss and you did not disappoint."

"I am glad I could help. Fear not, that angel has no more hold on your daughter."

LAKE OF EVIL

"Really, Harry? You are just going to sit there and watch us?"

"You don't know what horrors lurk below the surface, watching you from below and waiting for the right moment to drag you under."

Ragan rolled her eyes and tossed her paddleboard into the lake. The raven-haired beauty was expecting that type of response. Harry had been paranoid of water ever since watching *The Monster of Avery Lake* at the picture show. It was frightening, understandably, but it was just a film, after all.

"Fine, sit there and fry in the sun, then, see if we care," Jack remarked.

"A far better fate than becoming the next meal for some diabolical aquatic beast."

Janice smirked. "You really are something else, Harry. Enjoy the summer while it lasts. Before you know it, it will be too cold to swim or paddleboard and then you will regret it."

"I will live to see another summer and that is good enough for me," Harry responded.

The others shook their heads in disbelief and splashed their way into the lake with a chorus of laughter. Janice and Erin found the water too cold and attempted to ease their way in, ankle deep at first, and then to their knees. Jack thought them silly and jumped in, splashing them both and eliciting high-pitched squeals.

Harry sat in a lawn chair on the beach, keeping a healthy distance from the water. He felt that he was just far enough away to make good on his escape, if a lake monster emerged, seeking an easy meal. His friends, however, were doomed. They were just blissfully unaware.

All over the world, scientists had discovered pre-historic creatures that should have been dead billions of years ago, but somehow they had survived in the ocean's depths. These lakes were no different. This particular lake was even deeper than most. It was impossible for anyone to have explored the bottom. So, who knew what could be living down there since the beginning of time?

It was not unheard of for people to go missing in these parts. Harry knew there was something up with this lake. It was a lake of evil. The others teased him but he did not care. There were public pools when the urge to swim overcame him. It was not necessary to risk his life in the dark waters of the lake.

"Harry, why do you even come to the lake with us if you have no intentions of going in?" Agatha asked, after returning from the water and wrapping herself in a towel.

Why, indeed? Harry had to wonder. But what else

could he do on a hot summer's day? The best radio programs did not come on until the early evening. He did not possess enough money to sit at the malt shop every day. And besides, the few friends that he had were here at the lake. Maybe he felt it was his duty to keep an eye on them; to watch for strange ripples in the water or bubbles rushing to the surface, revealing a possible threat from below. Perhaps, he could shout a warning in time for his friends to get back to shore safely.

Harry shrugged a reply to the young girl, not willing to explain his reasons. They all thought him silly and a coward. Donald even accused him of being embarrassed about not being able to swim. He could swim, of course, just not in dangerous lakes.

This day was a particularly hot one and Harry walked over to the vendor who was selling snow cones out of a truck parked next to the beach.

"Be careful with that, son," the man in the truck said. "I hear lake monsters love snow cones."

Most of the regulars at the beach were aware of Harry's story by now. The man chuckled while Harry walked away, ignoring the jest. Harry didn't mind. Everyone was just ignorant to the dangers. That would be their undoing.

As Harry walked slowly back to his chair on the beach, something odd grabbed his attention from the corner of his eye. He spotted his friend Ragan on her paddleboard and she appeared to be in some type of distress. Harry ran closer to the water, though not too close, and squinted for a better look.

Ragan clearly appeared panicked and was frantically attempting to paddle away from something. Then Harry saw it too and his jaw dropped. His mind reeled. What was it? He swore it was a tentacle and it was moving toward his friend on the surface of the water. He could only imagine what nightmare that tentacle was attached to.

Ragan screamed out and Harry flew into action. He ran up and down the beach shouting that his friend was in trouble and someone needed to help her.

"Someone call the police!" he screamed. "The monster is going to get her!"

Folk who had been lounging lazily on the beach, all jumped up with fright. Panic overtook the beach and people scrambled about. Two gentlemen ran straight for the water and jumped in, swimming bravely toward the girl in grave danger.

Harry pointed to the snow cone vendor who had left his truck to see what all the commotion was about. "Don't just stand there, go get help! Call the police!"

When the concerned boy turned back to the dire situation in the water, he was surprised to notice everyone laughing. Even Ragan was laughing, albeit with a touch of embarrassment written upon her face. Jack was now holding the monster's tentacle aloft and that tentacle was nothing more than a long stick.

"I thought it was a snake," Ragan admitted.

The friends continued to laugh in the water for quite some time. The others on the beach were not too impressed and glared at Harry with angry eyes. Some of them had been blissfully asleep on their towels, until rudely awakened and put into panic mode. One woman even dropped the snow cone she had just purchased. Luckily for her, the man replaced it at no cost.

"A monster, eh?" the vendor shouted in Harry's

direction. "Call the police, eh? They need to arrest that stick before it causes anymore harm today."

Even Harry felt embarrassed, and when he returned to his lawn chair, he found that he had lost interest in consuming his snow cone. Soon enough, his friends ventured back to the beach to dry off and lay in the sun.

"Good thing Harry stands watch," Jack joked. "He will keep us all safe."

The others laughed.

"I appreciate it at least, Harry," Ragan said. "I could have sworn it was a snake."

"What did you think it was, Harry?" Agatha asked. "A giant squid? Some demon octopus?"

The others laughed some more.

"It's better to be safe than sorry," he finally replied. "Today it was a stick, tomorrow, who knows?"

The rest of that day passed uneventfully, along with the following week. One day, when it was mildly cool and Erin didn't feel much like getting into the chilly water, she hung back and sat with Harry in his usual spot on the beach. She had always found Harry to be a tad odd but harmless. They had all grown up in the same neighborhood and gone to school together. Erin felt sorry for Harry at times; he never seemed to have any fun.

"Harry, surely you have to know there are no monsters in the lake. How long have we all been coming here? Years, Harry, years. I have been swimming in there since my parents used to put floaties on my arms. Fish, Harry, there are just fish in there."

"You don't know that."

"Yes, I do. None of us have ever seen anything other than fish and none of us have ever been eaten."

"How many people have gone missing over the years? Quite a few."

"And?"

"What happened to all those people?"

"I don't know. Nobody knows. Runaways? God forbid, even a serial killer? But I am positive it was not a monster in the lake."

"I have kept newspaper clippings of everyone that has disappeared. All of their last known whereabouts were in this area, near the lake."

"So that means a monster took them?"

"Makes sense to me. There is never any trace of them, afterward. No clues at all. I bet whatever is left of them is at the bottom of that lake."

"Harry, police have searched the lake."

"The lake is too big and too deep. The police divers have never been able to search the deepest parts."

"Alright, but they went pretty deep and nothing ever ate those divers."

"Because the monster had just eaten. They were lucky."

"Ugh, you are impossible. Every summer you waste it away sitting here in your lawn chair, worrying."

"You will thank me when I spot something in time to save everyone."

"Like the stick that nearly ate Ragan?"

Harry blushed.

"Come on, go for a swim today."

"No."

"I will hold your hand, nothing will get you, I promise."

"No."

"I give up. A day will come when you look back at all the summers you wasted and regret it. I guarantee that."

The next weekend, the friends all went to a Saturday matinee at the picture show. A new film had just opened from the director, Otto Friedhelm, titled *Fangs*. It was the story of an overly large shark that was terrorizing the beaches along the southern coast. Not the best film, the others soon realized, to have brought Harry to see.

When the friends exited the theater, they were all forced to listen to Harry ramble on and on about the dangers of the lake and how that film had just reinforced all his deepest, darkest, fears. He was becoming increasingly difficult to be around. His paranoia was reaching epic levels and the others soon worried whether their strange friend might be suffering from a disease of the mind.

After watching *Fangs*, Harry now sat even farther away from the lake, with his chair nearly in the forest beside the beach. A pair of binoculars hung around his neck so that he could still watch his friends and keep an eye out for danger.

One warm afternoon, Jack joined Harry in order to retrieve a cold soda from their cooler. Jack never minded much that Harry would only ever sit and watch, because then he could also keep an eye on their coolers and clothes. The fact that Harry had been moving farther from the water and now sat with binoculars, though, was beginning to get people talking.

"You know, people are starting to talk about you."

"What do you mean?"

"Well, you sit here with binoculars. At a beach."

"So?"

"So, people think that is creepy. They think you are spying on girls with those."

"That's ridiculous, I am watching the water for trouble."

"Yeah, I get that. Your friends get that. The other people around here don't. All they see is a guy who comes to the beach all the time and never goes in the water. They see someone sitting way back here with binoculars and they think that is creepy."

"Yeah, but I am only...wait...what's that??"

Harry leaped up from his chair, gazing through the binoculars. Not far from Janice, something was just below the surface, and moving quickly toward her. Something dark and something about the same size as her.

"Oh, good heavens! Janice is in trouble! Look!"

He handed the binoculars to Jack who accepted them and took a look for himself. Jack shook his head and tossed the binoculars back to Harry.

"Maybe you should go sit in the shade, I think the heat has fried your brain."

Harry, feeling a touch perturbed that Jack was not as worried about their friend as he was, caught the binoculars and looked again. His shoulders slumped as he noticed another boy, near Janice, who had been snorkeling and swimming around under the water. He had just come up and removed his mask and snorkel. Jack left Harry alone and grumbled to himself all the way back to the water.

Harry, again, felt embarrassed. Even he was beginning to doubt himself now. What if he was just being too paranoid? What if it was just his over-active imagination? All these years he was positive a monster lived in that lake but was it possible that maybe he had been wrong?

Harry took Jack's advice and decided to get out of the sun and headed for the shade of the forest. He needed to walk and sort through his thoughts. There was immediate relief from the sun once he entered the forest. The leaves of the trees were full and effectively blocked much of the light.

Harry was no more than twenty feet in, when he heard a loud rustling sound behind him. Something was moving toward him and quite rapidly at that. He spun just in time to witness a blur of black fur and fangs reaching for him. The beast stood on two legs, much like a human, but was covered head to claw in black fur. It had pointed ears and fangs as long as his fingers.

Harry didn't even have time to scream, before the beast took him and he was never seen again. For much of his life, Harry worried about what lived beneath the surface of the lake and never once considered what lurked in the dark forest behind him.

GUT FEELING

It had been a long day of mostly paperwork and I was quite relieved to leave the office and breathe in the fresh summer air. I had almost forgotten what the world outside our musty records room smelled like. The sun was still out and it was a rare day indeed when I was able to leave work at a decent time.

I generally worked long grueling hours, which were not conducive to maintaining a relationship, thus, I was single. I needed to consider where I would stop for a bite to eat to quiet my angry stomach, given that there was nobody waiting for me at home.

"Excuse me, sir, but are you Detective Edward Kane?"

I turned to regard a lovely young woman with long dark hair. I would guess that she was somewhere in her twenties, and I was positive that I had seen her face somewhere before, but at the moment, I could not place it.

"Yes, ma'am, it is me. Have we met somewhere before? You seem familiar for some reason."

"No, Detective, we have not."

"How do you know me?"

"I have seen you in the papers a few times. You have been involved in some very bizarre cases over the years."

Wasn't that the truth. "I sure have. Was there something you needed?"

Her eyes darted back and forth, as if to ensure that there was nobody about to listen in on our conversation. She was visibly nervous.

"I was wondering if I could enlist your help in finding someone?"

"Well, usually you would file your case with the police and they will assign a detective to investigate. Have you spoken with the police?"

"They wouldn't listen to me."

"That doesn't sound right, are you…"

"They didn't want to listen to me, I swear it. But I really need some help."

"What about a private eye?"

"Please, Detective, I have read so much about you. If anyone can find this person, it would be you."

The woman appeared panicked; I could see it in her eyes. It was obvious to me that it meant a lot to her to locate whoever it was that was missing. I always had a good read on people, it was essential to my job. I could tell she was a kind and caring woman. She seemed educated and probably came from money, judging by her dress.

"Why don't you start by telling me who is missing?"

"He is just a friend."

"What is your friend's name?"

"Bernard."

"Bernard, what?"

"Just Bernard. I don't know his last name."

"He is your friend but you don't know his last name?"

"No, I don't. He never told me. We met a little over a year ago at the Big City Bus Terminal. He told me he was in some kind of trouble and until he knew me better, he could not reveal his last name."

"Where does he live?"

"I don't know."

"How would you keep in touch? Do you have a phone number?"

"No, I am sorry. We would just happen to bump into each other from time to time."

"So, you don't have a last name and you don't know where he lives? How do you know he is missing?"

"I just know it. I have not seen him around for over a month now. It is not like him. Like I said, he mentioned he was in some kind of trouble. People were after him. Bad people, I suppose. I fear they may have found him."

"What is your name, ma'am?"

"Amanda Finch."

The pause before she answered told me it was a fake name but I played along.

"Well, Amanda, you do not have much information to help anyone locate this man. He may not even be missing. You don't have a phone number or an address, so perhaps he has just moved on."

"No, something has happened to him, I just know it. I have this gut feeling that something is terribly wrong. Please, Detective, I beg you to help me."

"I need a coffee. How about we walk over to a diner and you can tell me more there?"

"I would rather not. Can we just talk somewhere more private?"

"Alright, how about Edgewood Park? It's just down the street there. We could find a bench."

"That would be fine."

"How about you go find a suitable bench and I will go grab a couple of coffees and meet you there shortly?"

"I could do that."

"What do you take in your coffee? It's on me."

"Oh, no thank you, Detective, none for me thanks."

"Are you sure?"

"Yes, but thanks for asking."

Amanda, or whatever her name was, left in the direction of the park and I walked to the nearest diner. I grabbed a coffee and a donut to go, and grumbled to myself over the thirteen cents I had to pay. Everything was just getting so damn expensive in the Big City, it was ridiculous.

I took my time in walking to the park, processing my interaction with the woman. I was definitely not getting the whole story but she was indeed desperate to find this man, that I was certain of. Now, I just had to figure out why. Jilted lover was my first instinct. I assumed Bernard never told her his last name or where he lived since he was most likely already married. He probably got whatever he wanted out of this "Amanda" and then disappeared back to his normal life. I was willing to bet that Bernard made her great promises, but of course, followed through with none of them.

And why the fake name? It occurred to me that

perhaps she was also married and wished to keep this as discreet as possible. Or perhaps she was a person of note within the Big City, which is why I had this strange feeling that I had seen her somewhere before.

Edgewood Park was quite large and I found Amanda sitting on a bench in a fairly secluded area of the park, overlooking a duck pond. I sat down beside her and sipped my coffee.

"As I have said, you have not given me much information, Amanda. Do you have any idea at all where Bernard could be?"

"He had a cabin just outside the city where he liked to spend most of his time."

"Now we are getting somewhere. Where is this cabin?"

"I don't know."

I sighed. "That doesn't help me much."

"He brought me there once, but I am terrible with directions. I could not tell you where it was at all. It was very dark when we went but if I had to guess, I would say it took us about forty minutes to get there."

"Forty minutes from where?"

"The bus terminal."

"He drove?"

"Yes."

"What kind of car does he have? Do you remember a plate number?"

"No, I am sorry. It was a dark-colored car and had four doors. That is all I remember."

This was a hopeless case. "Well, Amanda, how about you leave me with a description of Bernard. I can check to see if we have any reports of any missing Bernards, or anyone of interest fitting his description. Fair enough?"

She appeared devastated. "I suppose."

"It's all I can offer you right now. How can I get in touch with you?"

"I will just come find you in a couple of days to see if you have heard anything."

"It would be easier if I just called you or paid you a visit, if I find out anything worth reporting."

"That's ok, Detective, I will find you."

Amanda got up and walked away. Her head was down and she walked slowly, as if her shoes were filled with lead. I know she wanted a more positive reply from me but I just could not give one with so little to go on. She was withholding information, I was certain. For some reason she was afraid, or perhaps too embarrassed to tell me the full story.

I waited for her to disappear around a hill before following her. I thought if I found out where she lived, it might better help me to understand her situation. I kept a good distance between us and followed her out of the park and down Applefield Way. She walked at a snail's pace and I was getting frustrated. This was not exactly how I planned to spend my evening. It figures that the one day I left work at a decent hour, I would get caught up with something else.

It was dark by the time she entered the bus terminal and that's where I lost her. I was fairly confident in my ability to follow people without being noticed, but I had to wonder if she had spotted me and hid. I even asked an employee to check the women's restroom, but no luck. Amanda had vanished in the bus terminal and I was out of options.

I made the long walk back to the office where I had parked my car and returned home for the rest of the evening. The following day, I did investigate into any interesting reports involving anyone named Bernard, but found nothing. I also ran a check on Amanda Finch but found nobody by that name matching her apparent age. My strange encounter with Amanda soon left my mind as I became wrapped up once again with my ongoing cases.

Three days later, as I exited our office building, I ran into Amanda once more. I noticed she was wearing the same blue dress. Distress was plainly visible on her face.

"Did you find out anything at all?" she asked.

"No, I am afraid not. I have found nothing of interest concerning anyone named Bernard, or anyone fitting his description. You haven't given me much to go on, Amanda."

She began to weep. I attempted to place a hand on her shoulder for comfort but she turned and walked away. I shouldn't have felt so concerned but I did. There was definitely things she was not telling me but she was genuine in her desperation to find this man she believed missing.

"Amanda, wait. About this cabin, is there anything you can tell me about it at all? What did it look like?"

She turned and wiped away some tears. "Can we talk in the park?"

"Absolutely."

We returned to the same bench in the park and she did her best to recall any details about the cabin.

"I don't remember much about the outside of the cabin. It was very dark when we got there and still dark when we left. Inside, it had a kitchen and two separate bedrooms. It was fairly small."

"Alright, how about sounds? Was it near any water?"

"No, I don't remember hearing any water but I heard a train from time to time. It was faint, but definitely a train."

I rubbed my chin. "Well, you said it was about a forty-minute drive from the city. If you remember hearing a train then you could have been near Oakbridge. The Tanner Line runs east and west through there. Or perhaps Fernwood. The Blue Grass Express runs north and south through there. What about the drive? Do you remember anything about it? Smooth roads? Gravel roads?"

"I do remember the road sounding different at one point but it only lasted a minute or so. It sounded like we passed over a bridge."

"How long into your drive?"

"Maybe twenty minutes."

"Hmm, if you traveled twenty or so minutes west towards Oakbridge, you would cross the O' Connor bridge. Amanda, would you care to go for a drive? Perhaps it would help jog your memory."

"Yes, sure."

We walked back to my car and then headed west. It was late, so thankfully there was no traffic when leaving the city. As we approached the O' Connor bridge, I asked Amanda to close her eyes and listen while we passed over it.

"Yes," she said, excitedly. "That was what I heard."

"So, you reached this cabin roughly twenty minutes later?"

"I think so."

We drove for another ten minutes until there was a

fork in the road. I noticed several farms on the left-hand side, with many cattle roaming about the fields.

"Amanda, do you remember hearing any cows? Or perhaps smelling a farm?"

She shook her head. "No, I don't."

So I turned north, away from the farms. Shortly after, we arrived at a four-way intersection and I stopped. Bond Lake was to the east but Amanda did not recall being near to any water. The Tanner train line ran east and west just to the north of us. Amanda said the sound of the train was faint so I turned west instead of north. Several dirt roads branched off from the road we traveled on, and in the distance, a heavily wooded area sat on our right side.

"I do remember the road getting a little rough and bumpy before we stopped at the cabin."

I chose a dirt road and turned onto it. The road appeared to be seldom used and ran straight into the woods. It was a cloudy night to begin with, and when combined with the thick trees of the forest, the road would have been pitch-dark without the headlights from my car.

There were no cabins or cottages in this area of Oakbridge, as far as I was aware, but then again, I rarely had any reason to be out this way. I have had several picnics over at Bond Lake in the past, though, I was largely unfamiliar with this area.

We drove for a few minutes longer until the road ended. I grabbed a flashlight from my glove compartment and exited the vehicle.

"Did you have to walk very far from the car to the cabin? Do you remember?"

"Vaguely. It was perhaps five minutes."

Well, I had already come this far so there was no

sense in leaving now. The forest was as black as could be and all we could hear was a chorus of crickets. I chose a direction at random and plunged into the dense woods. I walked about for nearly ten minutes before I realized I was alone. Amanda must have gone back to the car, I imagined. The forest was too much for her to handle and she was not properly dressed for a hike in the woods.

I doubled back a ways and then chose a different direction, searching around some more. It wasn't my idea of a fun evening but I was committed. After another ten minutes, I was just about to head back to the car when I saw it. Faint lights in the distance where there shouldn't have been any lights.

I decided to investigate and crept as silently as I could toward the light. I exercised caution, in the event that whoever was out here, did not wish to be found. It was indeed a cabin, I soon realized. It was fairly small, about the size that Amanda had described. The windows were boarded shut but a definite light source emanated from inside.

For some reason, goosebumps ran their way up and down my arms. I touched the handle of my revolver within the shoulder holster inside my jacket, taking comfort that it was still there.

I left the cover of the forest and crept through a clearing, toward the front door. A twig snapped a few yards behind me and I whirled around to face a large, disheveled man, that fit the description of Bernard.

"Who are you?" the man demanded. "What are you doing here?"

I took note of the hatchet that he carried in his right hand.

"My car broke down a little ways away. I am lost and was looking for help," I decided to lie.

"You shouldn't be here."

"I would like to phone for a tow truck but if you don't have a phone in the cabin, I will be on my way."

"There is no phone here. Who else is with you?" he asked, looking around suspiciously.

"I am alone. It's just me. But I am leaving now, don't worry."

"You have already seen too much."

"Pardon me? I haven't seen anything. I will leave you to your privacy. Sorry for disturbing you."

"I can't let you leave."

The man suddenly ran towards me and raised the hatchet above his head. I quickly drew my revolver and shot him three times in the chest. He didn't immediately fall and actually continued to stumble forward. I backed up and fired two more shots. This time he went down and did not move again.

I kicked the hatchet away and nudged him with my foot. When he didn't move, I risked bending over and checked his pulse. He was dead. I stood and reloaded my gun as fast as possible. I had no idea who was inside that cabin.

I banged on the door and then stood back and pointed my gun. "This is Detective Kane. If there is anyone inside that cabin, exit slowly with your hands in the air."

There was only silence.

"We have the cabin surrounded. Come out with your hands up," I shouted once more.

After a few more moments of silence, I kicked the

door wide open and entered. An awful smell assaulted my nostrils immediately and I gagged. It was the unmistakable stench of death.

The kitchen and living area of the cabin was a disgusting mess. I covered my nose with a handkerchief and kicked open the doors to both bedrooms. The sight that awaited me will forever be burned into my mind. I discovered the bodies of five women. All were deceased. My jaw hung open in shock as I closely inspected the woman in a blue dress. She appeared to have only been dead a week and was the spitting image of Amanda. Even the dress was exactly the same. A twin? I wondered.

I hastily removed myself from that cabin of horrors. I had to get back to my car and radio for help. I had to check on Amanda. A million questions swirled around inside my mind. When I reached my car, I found that Amanda was nowhere in sight. Now, I am no tracker, but I could find no footprints, or any evidence of which way she may have gone. In fact, I found that only my footprints existed in a muddy area, where I remember distinctly that Amanda was with me.

I shook my head with confusion and waited for backup to arrive. An hour later, the cabin, along with the forest, was swarming with police and detectives. I soon found out why Amanda's face looked so familiar. Amanda was not Amanda Finch, as I had suspected. She was Amanda Jones and a photograph of her face hung in our office along with the four other women who had been missing for months. Amanda had been the last one to go missing and the last one to have been murdered.

Bernard's car was located not far away on a different road leading into the forest. A woman was found locked in the trunk of his car, still alive. She would have been victim number six, if I had not happened by.

I attempted to piece together this riddle in my mind but it made no sense at all. There was no trace, whatsoever, of the Amanda that helped me locate the cabin. It was as if she was a phantom. There were no footprints. There were no fingerprints. Nobody else had seen her except for me. My skin prickled at the notion that the ghost of Amanda had helped me track down her murderer.

My captain approached me. "Congratulations, Kane. This was one hell of a find. How did you know where to look?"

"Let's just call it a gut feeling."

EIGHTY-EIGHT BARNWOOD WAY

It was without a doubt, the creepiest house anyone had ever laid eyes upon. I can only imagine that the sole reason it was not condemned and torn down, was that the town officials were just as frightened by the witch that dwelled there as the children in the area were.

The two-story ramshackle house was located at the very end of Barnwood Way; a dead end street where the road was swallowed by the surrounding forest. During the summer months, while the leaves were thick on the trees, the house was not visible by any of the neighbors, and they were glad for that.

The exterior was in such a state of disrepair that none understood how the house had not yet collapsed upon itself, and yet, there it still stood. The paint was peeling. Shutters hung at odd angles. The eaves trough on the south side of the house had completely come loose and lay on the ground. And speaking of the ground, nothing grew within a twenty-foot radius of the house. Grass did not grow and the plants and trees nearest the home were dead and decayed.

That unsettling phenomenon was of course attributed to the curse of the witch. Black magic and foul rituals had ruined the land, everyone was certain of it. There was no other logical explanation. It was said that even animals shunned the area around the house, except for the large black crows which loved to perch on the roof. They were commonly believed to be the eyes of the witch, spying on those nearby.

Old Miss Hawthorn was as old as the hills for as far as anyone could tell. Nobody could remember a time when she did not live in town, and in that house, specifically. Her birthdate or even her place of birth was not on record. She had just always been a permanent fixture in Floral Green, a sleepy little rural town just west of the Big City. No husband. No children. Just her in that creepy old house on Barnwood Way.

I remember the first time I had ever seen Miss Hawthorn like it was just yesterday. I was in the fifth grade and at the grocery store with my mother one afternoon. I grew bored while my mother gossiped with another woman in the vegetable section, so I wandered off in search of sweets to drool over.

It did not take me long to find the jar of licorice sticks and I thought to go and beg my mother for a penny. It was then that a can of soup fell out of someone's basket and rolled toward me. I did the gentlemanly thing, of course, and picked it up in order to return it to its owner.

"Excuse me, ma'am, you dropped…"

My sentence was cut short as the elderly woman turned to regard me. My jaw dropped and the can of soup nearly fell from my grasp as I stared into the face of Old Miss Hawthorn. She had wrinkles upon wrinkles and her nose was long and crooked, sporting a wart on the end. Her snow-white hair appeared coarse and straw-like and stuck out from beneath her tattered black hat in odd angles. She smiled down at me and her teeth, the ones that were still left, were yellowed like old parchment.

I recall being frozen in place; paralyzed if you will, with fear. The stories about the witch claimed she ate children. Every story I had ever heard of Old Miss Hawthorn flashed through my mind while I stood only an arm's length away from this monster in human guise.

"Thank you, deary, I am so clumsy," she said with a hoarse voice, reaching for the can of soup that I still held.

The sound of her voice raised goosebumps all over my body, similar to listening to someone scrape their nails down a chalkboard. I smiled, stupidly, a vain attempt to mask my fear, and handed her the soup.

"And just what is your name?" she asked.

I opened my mouth but nothing came out. The thought also struck me that telling her my name was a bad idea. Perhaps my name would be used in some terrible spell or curse she could put upon me.

"Timmy, there you are."

NO, I silently screamed. My mother had just inadvertently given the witch my name. I was doomed, I knew it.

My mother also tensed up at the sight of the old hag. "Ah, come along now, Timmy, it's time to go."

Old Miss Hawthorn sighed and wore a disappointed expression on her aged face. She managed to flash me a weak smile as my mother pulled me away and dragged me to the closest cash register.

Later that evening, while I was reading funny books in bed with a flashlight, I replayed the encounter with the infamous witch in my mind. I figured if I survived the night without being turned into a frog or sprouting boils all over my skin, I should be alright.

And indeed I was alright the next morning and each morning that followed that. Life continued on as normal. In fact, when enough time had passed, my memory of Old Miss Hawthorn had faded completely, until years later when our paths crossed once more. I was riding my bike with three of my friends, when we found ourselves on Barnwood Way.

"I bet Rory is locked up in that witch's house," Bob commented, referring to Rory Baker, a boy our age who had gone missing a week prior.

"Nah, it's been a week already. Old Miss Hawthorn would have eaten him by now," Nick reasoned.

"We should go look around for clues," Fred suggested. "I don't think the police ever went there. Even they are afraid of the witch."

"I think that is a bad idea," I replied.

"Me too," Nick agreed. "You want us to be added to her menu?"

"Ah, come on. It's the middle of the afternoon. Witches are not active during the day, their powers are weak. They are only really dangerous at night," said Fred.

Nick, like the rest of us, was unconvinced. "Where did you hear that?"

"I read it in books. Witches draw their power from the moon. While the sun is out, she is just a frail old woman. Think of every picture you have ever seen drawn of a witch. It is always dark. They are always flying their broom through the night sky, passing over the moon."

Fred made a good point. Thinking back, I had never seen a drawing of a witch that was out during the light of day. It was always a night scene.

"We could just go look around the property. Maybe we could find something of Rory's as a clue," he added.

I shook my head in disagreement, as I was still against the idea. Fred's logic won over my other friends, though, and I was out-voted. Not wishing to be labeled a coward, I followed the others to the creepy old house at the end of Barnwood Way. Even during the light of day, the sight of that house unnerved me; unnerved us all.

The house was surrounded by a thick forest but nothing grew near to the house at all. It looked every bit like a house taken from the horror films that we occasionally watched at the picture show. The four of us cautiously laid our bikes on the ground, facing them in the opposition direction of the house, in case a speedy getaway was required, then slowly creeped about.

"What are we even looking for?" I whispered, wanting nothing more than to be away from there.

"Anything out of the ordinary," Fred replied.

"Everything here is out of the ordinary," Bob correctly countered.

Fred shook his head. "We know Old Miss Hawthorn never had any kids. So let's see if we can find anything around here that might belong to any of the missing kids she kidnapped and ate."

I swallowed hard. That was a most displeasing image that Fred had just forced into my delicate mind. I imagined a giant woodstove in a dark basement, filled with cobwebs. And there was Old Miss Hawthorn, cackling away over a cauldron, while waiting for her latest victim to cook inside the stove. Needless to say, I tried very hard to expel that image and hung back closer to our bikes. If the witch came out of her house, I wanted a better head start than the others.

"Hey, look at all these frogs," shouted Bob, from the right side of the house. "There must be about twenty of them."

I positioned myself in a spot where I could see where Bob stood but I was still closer than everyone else to our bikes. Bob stooped over a muddy pond and the others joined him. I kept one eye on Bob and my other on the decrepit front door to the house.

"I bet these are some of those kidnapped kids," Fred blurted, a little louder than I thought he should have.

"That's ridiculous," Nick countered. "They are just frogs."

"Witches turn people into frogs and then use their parts in awful recipes or as components for spells. Makes eating them easier too."

Bob jumped back from the pond; his face was as pale as a ghost. "Maybe we should go now. I think I have seen enough of this place."

I breathed a giant sigh of relief when Nick agreed. They began making their way back, quite quickly I might add, to where I awaited by the bikes. Then, to my ultimate horror, I watched in slow motion as Fred picked up a rock and launched it at a second-story window. Time slowed down as I watched that rock sail through the air and then crash through the window.

We scrambled to get on our bikes, bumping into each other and knocking each other over, like a slapstick skit from a film featuring the Four Imbeciles. I even punched Fred in the arm, so angry was I that he had put us all in jeopardy. I thought it could not get any worse, when my shoe lace became caught on my bike's pedal. My friends were off and racing away while I struggled to get myself free.

"My hat!" Fred yelled, with panic clearly evident in his voice. "Timmy, grab my hat!"

At some point during all the commotion, Fred had lost his favorite red hat. He never went anywhere without that hat, and in fact, he looked fairly odd to the rest of us anytime he was made to remove it. There it sat in the dirt, a few feet away from me.

I cursed myself for my kindness. As I finally freed my lace, I dove and grabbed the hat before turning back to my bike. That's when I heard that voice again. That same voice that was like fingernails on a chalkboard and it took me right back to that encounter in the grocery store. I froze in place like a statue.

"You there. What is this about?"

For some reason, in my child's mind, I thought if I just remained still and did not answer, she would not notice me and go away. I was wrong.

"Well? Answer me."

I slowly turned. My friends were gone and out of sight, and the feeling of dread threatened to stop my heart and kill me right then and there. Old Miss Hawthorn stood in her front door with her hands placed angrily on her hips.

"I-I-I…well…w-w-we…," I stammered.

"I remember you. Your name is Timmy, isn't it?"

Oh good heavens! She remembered my name!

"Y-yes, ma'am."

"What were you boys doing here?"

"Ah…well…w-we were j-just riding our b-bikes in the area and somehow ended up h-here." Then I hastily added, "I didn't throw the r-rock."

"I know, it was that other boy, the trouble maker."

"Y-yes, it was Fred who did it," I blurted, and did not care one bit about being a snitch. Fred would have done the same if the situation was reversed.

I shivered at the thought that she had been watching us this whole time. I could have sworn I scanned every window for faces. Then I spotted a crow perched on the roof and remembered that folk said the crows acted as her eyes.

"You punched the other boy, too. Why?"

"W-well I was mad that he threw the r-rock. I didn't know he w-would d-do something like that. I am v-very sorry."

She waved me away. "Run along, Timmy. And tell your friend, Fred, he is not welcome around here."

"Y-yes, ma'am."

I could not get out of there fast enough. My friends were nowhere in sight and I found out later that they just assumed I was captured so did not stick around. You certainly learn what your friends are really like when faced with a witch crisis.

Fred, of course, was deeply upset that I told her his name. I explained I could not be held accountable for anything said, since everyone left me behind. I had even saved his hat, for which he was most grateful.

That very next summer, though, Fred went missing. He had left Nick's house one evening, sometime before midnight, but had never made it home. Posters went up everywhere and police combed the neighborhoods. Nick stopped by my house later that second night, holding two flashlights.

"Come on, let's go join in the search for Fred."

"Where would we even look that the police have not already tried?" I wondered.

"Old Miss Hawthorn's place."

"Pardon me? Surely you are kidding."

"It has to be her. She wanted Fred for breaking her windows."

"That's nonsense. That was a year ago."

"Well, he had apparently done it a few more times since. He always told me that if he ever went missing, to make sure I went to Hawthorn's place to look for him."

"But, it's so dark out."

He handed me the flashlight. "Yeah, so I am not going alone. Take that and let's go. Look, it hasn't even been twenty-four hours yet. If he is there, we could be in time to save him."

Nick had a point. I was not sure how long it took before a witch devoured her captive but it somehow made sense that it was not done immediately. Age had made me braver, or dumber, perhaps. While butterflies still flew around my stomach at the thought of visiting the witch's house at night, I still followed Nick down the driveway.

We got on our bikes and approached the dead end of Barnwood Way, not more than twenty minutes later. We decided to ditch the bikes farther from the house and then creep in on foot. If we had thought her property was frightening during the day, words could not describe how terrifying it was at night. And eerily silent, we both noted. Even the chirping of crickets was absent.

As we exited the forest and made our way across the muddy expanse toward the house, I quickly scanned for any crows perched on the roof. Birds were generally not seen at night and tonight was no exception. I don't know why that made me feel so much better but I figured there was less of a chance for the witch to be alerted to our presence.

The front of the house was dark and appeared devoid of life. Nick tugged on my sleeve and I followed him around the back of the house. It was there that we spotted a light source from a first floor window. The window was covered with an old worn curtain but there was enough of a gap to allow someone to peek inside. Nick pointed to the window and I nodded, indicating for him to lead the way and I would follow. My heart thumped in my chest and I was sure that even my friend could hear it.

I followed him toward the window, albeit a little slowly. He looked back and motioned that he was going to peek in. Again, I nodded. As he did his best to move as silently as possible, I took note of the strange patch of straw that covered the ground in front of the window. I crept in for a closer examination.

Nick paid the straw patch no heed and placed his face against the glass of the window to peer inside.

"No, Nick, wait," I said desperately, trying to keep my voice to a whisper.

It was too late. Nick's full weight caused the straw

patch to give way and he vanished into the ground. I reached for him but he was gone before I could grab onto anything. Unfortunately, I was now off balance and also tumbled into the pit that had been previously hidden.

Somehow, I managed to latch onto the lip of the hole and there I dangled; my fingers dug deeply into the earth, holding on for my dear life. Below, I heard Nick groan.

I hazarded a look below me and the hole led straight into what appeared to be a cellar beneath the house. A light source came from a burning fire; a fire that sat below a large black cauldron. Beside that cauldron, stood Old Miss Hawthorn, dressed head to toe in black. She held a large jar in her withered hands and the contents of the jar nearly stopped my heart. Inside was a frog, but not just any frog. It was a frog that wore a little red hat. A tiny version of Fred's favorite hat.

"My leg," Nick moaned below me on the cellar floor. "I think I broke my leg."

Old Miss Hawthorn cackled and that cackle nearly stole the strength from my arms and forced me to let go. Some inner-strength I did not even know I possessed, allowed me to hang on.

She flashed a wicked smile my way. "Your friend on the floor there is now mine, Timmy. Now, be gone from here and never let me see you again. And if you tell anyone about what you have seen, I can promise you that you will be next."

That was all I needed to hear. I was suddenly imbued with the strength of Hercules as I climbed out of that hole. Her horrible cackle chased me through the forest and even down the street. I ran right past my bike, not wishing to waste any time in picking it up. I ran and ran and ran. Just when I did not think I was able to run anymore...I ran some more.

IN DESPERATE NEED OF PRAISE

Butterflies flitted about in my stomach. I was about to give the most important performance of my life, so naturally, I was nervous to the point of vomiting. I waited backstage and paced back and forth, wearing a path into the wooden floor. I dared to take one final peek around the curtain and excitedly observed that it was a full house. Mind you, the venue was quite small but there was not an empty seat to be found.

Admittedly, the Big City housed many grand theaters that could have served my purpose but there had always been a certain charm about The Emerald Theater. True, it had been abandoned for years, but I had spent months, painstakingly fixing it up for my big show. And to my credit, I had done it all on my own. I had no help, whatsoever. This was going to be a solo performance. A daunting task that I had never before attempted.

From the time I was a young lad, I had wanted nothing more in life than to be a stage performer. I started out with school plays as a teen and then slowly progressed to more elaborate productions. There were many theaters throughout the Big City but every performer, without doubt, dreamed of working on the big stages in the theater district, or at one of the large casinos. That is when you knew you had made it. The whole city watching you. Journalists. Critics. Everyone.

For years, I was part of the Flying Flamingo troupe. We performed a wide variety of different plays, ranging from serious dramas, all the way to outrageous comedies. I was having the time of my life and we had met with some mild successes. Two years ago, our group was invited to perform at the very prestigious Grand Royal Theater. It was our shot at the big time. It was the goal we had been working our whole lives to achieve and we flopped.

The media blasted us. We had performed a touching tale of two lovers but the Big City Times titled their review, A Horror Show. Other papers and magazines similarly ripped us to shreds, calling us amateurs and a waste of good money. I truly felt I gave the performance of my life and it was my colleagues who had caused us to flounder on stage. Several critics, though, had singled me out in reviews, naming me as the weakest link. My name was dragged through the muck of the city's gutters. I was devastated.

Shortly thereafter, I had a falling out with the rest of the group and was expelled for reasons I would rather not get into. They can say whatever they want about me. They can tell as many lies as they like but I was going to quit anyway. They were a bunch of immature whiners who only brought me down. My performances and my good name were tarnished by their lack of acting skills and professionalism. I should have left them long ago. I am on a level far above them all and did not need them in the slightest.

I have now spent the last year writing my own original play. A tragic tale of a misunderstood man. Someone with so much potential but never accepted by those around him. The story consists of several different characters, of which I have elected to play all, myself. I will be damned if I allow the incompetence's of others to ruin this night for me. Tonight is my night to shine, alone. Tonight, I elevate myself to stand above all other performers. Tonight, nobody will be able to deny my thespian talents.

It was almost time to begin and my level of nervousness was through the roof. It was not going to be easy running a one-man show, but I envied those performers who could pull it off. People like the ventriloquist, Sullivan, of Sullivan and Micky. Magicians like, The Great Fazoo. Their shows lived or died by their performance, alone. They had nobody else to rely on if the going got rough. But I knew that I could do this. I had trained my entire life for this. That crowd out there was in for a real treat.

ACT 1, SCENE 1

(Stage lights off except for the spotlight on center stage. Rufus walks into the light with head down and opens with a soliloquy.)

RUFUS: I don't know why people don't understand me. I don't feel as though I am all that different from everyone else. Is it because I am a recluse? Because I don't often socialize with others? Has anyone ever stopped to consider why I don't care to socialize? Maybe it is society that has molded me into the person that I am. The ridicule. The whispers behind my back. The sneers. People treat others like outsiders and then wonder why they behave the way that they do. Thinking back, though, perhaps my mother may have played some small part.

I attached fishing line to several of the light switches and subtly tugged on one to turn off the spotlight, casting the theater into total darkness. I had memorized the walk from center stage to back behind the curtain, so even without the use of my eyes, I made it unhindered.

I quickly changed into my next costume and was quite proud of myself for the ingenuity of it. The left side of my body was dressed as Rufus' mother and the right side of my body was dressed as a young Rufus. Now, I could stand on stage and carry on a conversation between two people, by simply switching my stance. I flipped on two stage lights and went back out. Rufus' mother was facing the audience.

ACT 1, SCENE 2

(Dorothy enters. Stamps foot on floor while making the motion of knocking on a door.)

DOROTHY: Rufus? Rufus? You open the door this instant. Rufus? I know you are awake, I can see the light from your lamp under the door.

(Rufus turns to audience. Unlocks the door.)

DOROTHY: I knew it! You were reading those awful magazines again. You are filling your fool head with nonsense. Monsters, Rufus? Really? Those monster magazines are pure rubbish.

(Dorothy makes the motion of ripping the magazines.)

DOROTHY: There! That takes care of that! There will be no more reading in this room. Do you hear me? Bedrooms are for sleeping in. If your father was still around you'd get the belt, mark my words. But disobey me again and see what happens. Don't push me.

RUFUS: But, Mom, there is nothing wrong with those magazines.

DOROTHY: NO MORE READING! (Dorothy shouts and raises her hand in a threat.)

Then I did something that no stage actor should do. I hazarded a glance at the audience to gauge their reactions, thus far. An actor should focus on the task at hand. A really good actor gets lost in the role and is not even aware that there is an audience present. The audience can be a distraction if one tends to overly worry about how they perceive the performance. A negative reaction could have a profound effect on an actor and jeopardize the show. I truly felt I could take the risk, though. I needed to see their faces, as they had been fairly quiet to this point.

The first face I recognized, sitting in the front row, was William Freeman. He worked for the Daily Globe and had trashed my last performance. He said that his child in kindergarten could have done a better job than I did. His face was difficult to read. I moved on to the next.

In the row directly behind William, I noticed Nancy Blain. She wrote a column for the Venus Tribune. She had said she would have walked out of that performance, if she was not getting paid to be there in order to write a review. Her eyes were wide. Wide with wonder? Wide in awe of the show so far?

To her left was Neil Bradshaw. He wrote reviews for Global Entertainment and said that I had single-handedly brought down that last show. Now he was witnessing how I could single-handedly carry an entire show. He was stone-faced for the moment but I was sure that would all change by the second act.

I found Donald Donaldson among the crowd. He was a reporter for BCTV news on the television. I had never owned a picture tube but I had heard that he referred to my acting as pure rubbish. He sat there wearing a poker face. Perhaps it was too early to gauge their opinions.

Before finishing the current scene, I spotted Barry Addams. He was probably the biggest deal of them all. He reviewed movies and plays for the Big City Times. Of course, he sat dead-center in the middle of the theater, having the best view. He would be the toughest nut to crack. He loathed my performance in that last show and had said the most hurtful things. He did not appear too impressed at the moment. I would need to step up my game.

ACT 2, SCENE 2

(Children walking about in the schoolyard.)

KID 1: Hey, look. It's weirdo Rufus.

KID 2: Weirdo Rufus. Weirdo Rufus.

KID 1: Is he talking to one of his imaginary friends again?

KID 2: He must be, cuz nobody else wants to be friends with such a weirdo.

Much of Act Two focused on the steady decline in Rufus' social life. At home, his mother pretty well had him confined to his bedroom, where even the simple act of reading was strictly prohibited. So, he did indeed invent imaginary friends to talk and play with, in order to pass the time away. At school, he kept to himself and tried to avoid the other kids whenever possible. The only thing he enjoyed about school was drama class. In drama class, he could pretend to be other people and could leave the life of Rufus behind, even if it was for only a short while. He grasped at any opportunity he could to escape.

Act Three jumped ahead several years and now

portrayed Rufus as a lonely young man. After the untimely death of this mother, he truly had nobody left. He found it difficult to hold down jobs for any length of time. People thought him strange and socially awkward. His life had no purpose until he joined an acting troupe. Now, he could escape being Rufus once more. Now, he could be anyone but Rufus.

Acting yielded a paycheck but it was not much. It afforded him a tiny apartment in the slums of the Big City; a neighborhood that was referred to as the Junkie Jungle. Despite his surroundings, Rufus never partook in any illicit activities and even refused to imbibe any alcoholic beverages. He still did not socialize outside of his acting group, and even within it, conversations were kept to the work at hand. He had no desire to discuss his life outside the theater.

As the third act came to a close, I pulled the string that would darken the stage and once again allowed myself a moment to study the audience. Wide-eyed and stone-faced, still. All of them. I suppose I could understand. The content thus far had been fairly deep and somewhat depressing. The plight of Rufus would tug at the heartstrings of any feeling individual. The fourth act would see a change in tempo. The fourth act allowed for a bit of comedy and wit on the part of Rufus. Now, I would showcase my comedic abilities after dazzling them with my dramatic skills.

During the second scene of the fourth act, I launched several clever quips but could not elicit any change in expression from the audience. Not a single laugh. Not even a mild chuckle. I can admit it was quite disheartening. Scene three provided me with the best joke yet and still the room remained silent. I was convinced these critics possessed no sense of humor, whatsoever. That was quite evident. The fourth act closed with Rufus earning chastisement by critics for perhaps his greatest performance on stage. Their verbal and written barbs caused tremendous damage and attributed to the actor departing from the group. Without acting in his life, Rufus walked a dark path, while harboring even darker thoughts.

Act Five was the final act, consisting of a single scene. It also included the most elaborate costume yet. If nothing else had impressed the critics to this point, then my Grim Reaper costume was sure to inspire a sense of awe. I wore a long and flowing robe of black, with a frightening mask that transformed my face into a grinning skull with glowing red eyes. In my right hand I carried a long scythe.

ACT 5, FINAL SCENE

(Theater goes dark. One single light on stage. Grim Reaper appears through a cloud of smoke to deliver final speech.)

GRIM REAPER: And now, my friends, we come to the end. The end of the line for poor Rufus. Rufus will suffer no more at the hands of idiotic critics. Those bitter men and women who could obviously not act, themselves, so choose to write about it instead. Choosing to lambaste those hard-working individuals who poured their entire souls into their craft. To belittle those that they look down upon. No more, my friends.

No more.

With my left hand, I produced a book of matches. The lack of empathy from the audience for the fate of Rufus disgusted me. I had not noticed one single smile from any faces, for the entire show. Not even a nod of approval. They should have been astounded by this night's performance. I could not fathom any one of them ever seeing anything as marvelous before. What other actor could pull off an entire play by themselves? None, that's who. Well, to Hell with these critics. To Hell with them all, quite literally.

Before I could strike a match, a loud thump came from a side door, just to the right of the stage. It startled me and I momentarily lost my train of thought.

"Who would dare interrupt the final scene?"

*   *   *   *

Several officers burst into the decrepit old theater, once the battering ram made short work of the barred side door. Upon spotting the lone actor on stage, they raised their revolvers and took aim. One of the new arrivals, wearing a long brown trench coat, took in the scene around him and shook his head in bewilderment. He too, pointed his gun at the actor.

"Drop the broomstick and put your hands in the air," the man shouted. "My name is Detective Edward Kane and you are going to want to do exactly what I tell you."

A uniformed officer sniffed the air, curiously. "Ah, Detective? I smell gasoline."

Detective Kane made the same horrendous discovery

and then his eyes went wide as he noticed the book of matches in the strange man's hands. This entire theater was ready to go up in flames.

"Drop the matches, NOW!"

The man on the stage had his face painted with white makeup. Sweat was causing the makeup to run down his face. It dripped onto the black garbage bag he wore, with holes punched through for his arms. He threw down the broomstick he held in one hand but kept ahold of the matches.

"I am not playing any games here. Drop the matches," Kane demanded.

The strange man frowned. These officers had ruined his finale. The Grim Reaper was to transform the entire theater into the final set, Hell. Rufus was going to Hell and he was going to take those ungrateful critics with him.

No matter, he thought to himself, the police would just have to join him.

BLAM! BLAM!

The man attempted to strike a match and Detective Kane shot him twice in the chest. He stumbled about, as if enacting a dramatic death scene, and then dropped the matches and fell to the stage.

The officers held their breath, expecting the sparks from Kane's revolver to ignite the theater, but luck was with them and nothing had happened.

Kane exhaled and again took in the scene around him. "Jones, see if he is dead. The rest of you untie everyone and see if anyone is injured."

The detective approached the nearest audience member and removed the woman's gag. "What in the hell was going on here?" he asked, while untying her wrists from the arms of the chair.

"That raving lunatic kidnapped us all and held us hostage. He forced us to watch his horrible last performance. I have never seen anything this bad in my entire life. Words can't even describe the insanity we just sat through."

Officer Jones approached the bleeding man on stage and noticed his shallow breathing. He leaned over the fallen actor who was attempting to speak.

"Did they like the show? What are they saying down there? Was it the best they have ever seen?"

The man closed his eyes and breathed his last breath.

FAIRBROOKE: HOME FOR SENIORS

"Welcome to Fairbrooke, Doctor O'Hara. I believe this place is much smaller than what you are used to but I trust you will enjoy it here."

I smiled and nodded. "Thank you, Miss, ah, Miss…"

"Mrs. Shay."

"Thank you, Mrs. Shay. Yes, this is certainly a drastic change from the Big City General Hospital but a welcomed one. I look forward to a more relaxed environment."

"Well, we may not have many residents here yet, but the ones we do have can be demanding at times. Nothing serious, really, but they do so love to complain."

"Complainers I can handle."

Mrs. Shay smiled. "You say that now." Then she lowered her voice. "Speak of the devil. Here comes one of our resident hypochondriacs now. Henry Briar has something different wrong with him each week."

Henry Briar shuffled toward us, obviously displaying a pain in his legs. He was tall and lean, and I soon learned was eighty-eight years old.

"Good afternoon, Mister Briar, how are you feeling today?" Mrs. Shay asked.

"Oh, it's my legs. A terrible pain in both my legs. I fear I shall lose my ability to walk, I just know it."

"Well, Mister Briar, I am Doctor O'Hara and I will be working here from now on. How about I stop by your room this afternoon and we will have a look at those legs?"

"You can come by but there won't be anything you can do. You'll probably need to saw them off. Probably infected that's what's wrong, I just know it."

Henry shuffled off down the hall, grumbling to himself as he went.

"Last week it was his left shoulder. The week before that his right eye," Mrs. Shay told me.

"I will examine him later and see what I can find out."

The two of us walked through a lounge area and I was introduced to another resident.

"Good morning, Mrs. Henson. This is our new doctor, Doctor O'Hara."

"Pleasure to meet you, Doctor. Maybe you can do something about my chest pain before I die. The last doctor was useless and couldn't do anything for me."

"I would be happy to give you an examination this afternoon, once I am settled."

"Mrs. Henson is always dying. She has been here just over a year and a half and has been dying, according to her, every day since her arrival," Mrs. Shay explained, as she escorted me to my new office. "Here you go, this is your office. I would suggest you keep your door closed or you will have everyone in here at all times, complaining about their problems."

I thanked her and set about organizing my new office and making it feel more like mine. I hung a few certificates and awards on the wall, and displayed a photo of my wife and two kids on the desk. Several other staff members dropped by to introduce themselves and welcome me to Fairbrooke.

I found myself enjoying a moment of silence, which was not something I had while working at the Big City General. The pace there was fast and exhausting. It was an environment better suited to the younger doctors. I put in my time there, twenty-three years to be exact, now I deserved a little break and looked forward to a more relaxed environment.

Later that day, I looked over Mister Briars legs, and as was suggested by Mrs. Shay, I could find nothing wrong.

"But I can barely walk," he told me. "The pain is terrible."

I was informed that last week he was saying the same thing about his left shoulder. "How does your shoulder feel, Mister Briar? I was told that you were having problems with it last week."

"Ah, well, it seems fine now. But it will flare up again, you can bet on that."

"How about I get you a walker to help you move around? And I will keep a close watch on those legs in the meantime."

"The last few doctors couldn't do a damn thing for

me either. A bunch of useless quacks, I say," he grumbled.

"I just don't see anything wrong with your legs. Let's give it a few more days to see if they get better on their own."

"It will be too late in a few days. I will lose both my legs."

I left Mister Briar's room and asked one of the nurses' to have a walker brought by to help him in the meantime. As with most hypochondriacs, they could convince themselves that something was wrong. His legs may be perfectly fine, but he has created this pain in his mind, so for him it is very real.

I made the short trek over to the room of Mrs. Henson and gave her a thorough examination with the same results. She complained of a pressure on her chest which was making it difficult for her to breathe. She was certain that the reaper of death was knocking at her door. I could find nothing to suggest there was a problem with her chest or her breathing.

"I think you will be staying with us a lot longer than you think, Mrs. Henson."

"I don't see how. I can barely breathe. Tonight is probably going to be my last night here. Will you phone my children and inform them?"

"Hmm, maybe we should not alarm them so soon, huh? I have been doing this doctoring thing for quite some time now and in my expert opinion you are going to live."

Soon after, I met with Mister Seagal, who said the pain in his right hand was so great that he could not even move his fingers. Then Mrs. Ruttle dropped by my office, complaining of an intense headache that would not go away, no matter what pills she took.

I, of course, could find nothing to suggest that any of these people suffered from any afflictions. In my experience, I found that many of the lonely seniors in these homes were just looking for attention. Perhaps, they had no family to fuss over them so they sought the attention elsewhere.

One evening, when most of the residents were asleep, I stayed late in my office and poured through the records left behind by the previous doctors. Mister Briar had complained of something different nearly each week, and as expected, nothing was ever truly wrong. Once a doctor determined that he was fine, he just moved on to a different body part and began the whole complaining process anew.

Mrs. Henson was always dying, in her mind, from one excuse to the next. Mrs. Ruttle, who came to me with a terrible headache, only recently complained about a terrible pain in her back, which was determined to be nothing as well.

I could see from the notes made by the other doctors that they were frustrated and growing rather irritable from the constant phantom complaints. Over the next few days, I made some inquiries and discovered that the last four resident doctors before me had all quit. Apparently the folk here had driven them out.

One afternoon, I sat in a lounge area and questioned Mrs. Shay. "How did the residents get along with the previous doctors?"

"They weren't too fond of them, I would say."

"I have found that seniors can be rather stubborn at times. I wonder if perhaps they did not like any of the other doctors, so decided to force them out?"

"What do you mean?"

"Well, I have been reading over a lot of notes and could feel the growing frustration that these doctors were feeling. They all quit, did they not?"

"Yes, that is correct."

"So, my theory is that the residents decided to drive these doctors crazy with phantom afflictions, until they were forced to leave. Perhaps, these doctors were not giving them the proper attention that they felt they deserved."

"Hello, Doctor. Hello, Mrs. Shay. Care for some apple pie? Baked fresh today," a small woman with short white hair said.

The woman held a tray with a warm, freshly-baked apple pie, that smelled wonderful.

"Thank you, Mrs. Walters, we would love some pie," Mrs. Shay replied.

The elderly woman smiled and placed the pie on a table and walked away. I had not met this woman yet and surprisingly, she did not come to me with any complaints.

"Mrs. Walters, you said?"

"Yes, such a sweet woman and always baking things. Her pies are fantastic."

"She doesn't complain of any pains or say that she is going to die?"

"No, actually she says very little at all. Spends most of her time in her room baking."

"You see, this supports my theory. Mrs. Walters bakes and everyone enjoys what she makes. She gets attention from that and is satisfied. She does not have to make something up in order for people to fuss over her."

"You may have a point. No other doctor has ever

found anything wrong with anyone here, aside from the normal effects of aging."

I returned to my office and pondered an idea I had rolling around inside my mind. If the residents wanted to play games then I could play one of my own. If all they wanted was attention then I would give it to them. I feel that the other doctors failed because they dismissed all the phantom ailments as being just that. They were telling these people that they were wrong. That was not the reaction the residents were looking for. I decided I would play along with their personal diagnoses and attempt to treat them.

I made a phone call to a pharmacist friend of mine and placed an order for some harmless vitamins that would act as a placebo. Maybe if I could convince folk that these pills were treating their pain, they would believe it and it would have the desired effect.

My shipment arrived a few days later and I paid a visit to Mister Briar's room. I planned to begin with him and quickly started examining his legs.

"They are still hurting you, are they?"

"Tremendously. You are going to have to cut them off, won't you? There must be some kind of infection that you cannot detect."

"Actually, I notice some swelling here. Yes, yes indeed. I believe this is your problem."

Mister Briar appeared shocked.

"Really? You mean you can see something wrong?"

"Yes, most definitely. It is only a slight swelling, which is why I must have missed it before. But there is definite swelling and would contribute to the pain and trouble you are experiencing while walking."

"Can anything be done about it?"

"Of course, this is very treatable. I just happen to have a pill that will reduce the inflammation and remove the pain within an hour." I searched around inside a small black bag I carried with me. "Ah, yes, here it is. Now, Mister Briar, take one of these with some water after your next meal. This should make you feel much better."

"Umm, ok, well if you say so."

"Yes, I will check on you first thing in the morning."

I was most excited to see how this miracle pill was going to work and went in search of Mister Briar, as my shift began the next morning. I found him up and about in the hallways, without the use of his walker.

"Good morning, Mister Briar. How are you today?"

"My legs feel fine. No more pain. You did it. I can't believe you really did it. You must be the world's best doctor."

I smiled. "Thank you, but I am nowhere near the best. But I am so happy you are feeling better."

"None of the other doctors ever believed me. They said the pain was all in my head. My head, can you believe that?"

"I suppose they did not examine you as thoroughly as they should have."

"Quacks. All of them."

I proceeded to track down Mister Seagal and repeated the same process, finding some swelling on this right hand which did not actually exist, and prescribing the same placebo. I checked back with him much later that afternoon and was pleased to find the pain in his hand had completely disappeared. As with Mister Briar, Mister Seagal went on and on about the incompetence of the other doctors and praised me for believing him and fixing his problem.

I was now satisfied that I could treat the rest of the residents here with the same pill. I was truly convinced that pretending to believe in them was the key to this plan's success. Elderly folk did not want to be constantly told that they were crazy and imagining things. Once I got on their good side, I believed things would change around here. I would try to give them the attention they deserved, to prevent any more mystery ailments.

The next morning, as I was about to leave my office in search of Mrs. Ruttle with the awful headaches, Mister Briar entered. He was holding his throat and looked quite distressed.

"What's wrong, Mister Briar?"

"My throat," he croaked. "Hurts to swallow and I can barely talk."

I sighed. The pain in his legs was gone so now he had a pain in his throat. Mrs. Shay had warned me of this. I examined his throat, and of course, there was no redness or inflammation. There was no indication at all that his throat should be in pain.

"It's bad, isn't it?" he asked, after I finished my exam. "This will be the end of me, won't it?"

"Your throat is very red," I lied. "But I have another pill that should clear this right up."

"That looks just like the other one for my legs."

"True, they look alike, but I assure you this one is made specially to deal with throat pain. Trust me, it should do the trick."

"Well, alright, if you say so," he whispered.

Mister Briar accepted the pill and left my office.

Shortly, thereafter, Mister Seagal marched in.

"I can't move the fingers in my left hand now!"

"Hmm, but your right hand is fine, is it?"

"Yes, no pain at all. But now I have the exact same pain in my left hand. What's wrong with me, Doc?"

"It is very common for the pain to switch hands. I was expecting this. You will just need another pill and this time it will eliminate your pain completely."

"I am left-handed. I am useless without my left hand!"

"Just take this pill and I promise you will regain the use of your hand."

With the departure of Mister Seagal, I tracked down Mrs. Henson, who was listening to the Jungle Johnny program on the radio. I gave her the same pill and told her it would help her chest pain and she would soon be able to breathe normally. Later, I found Mrs. Ruttle sitting outside and prescribed her the pill for her terrible headaches.

To my total dismay, they were all complaining of the same symptoms the following day. I did not know what went wrong. My plan seemed to be working.

"I still can't breathe, I am going to die today," Mrs. Henson said.

"My head feels like it will explode," Mrs. Ruttle added.

"I can't swallow," Mister Briar complained.

And of course, Mister Seagal could not move the fingers on his left hand. I really had no other option but to prescribe them all another pill and send them on their way.

I sat alone in my office and ran through everything in my mind. I thought I had them all figured out. Could I have been wrong? I thought that believing in them and prescribing them the placebo would have worked. Mister Briar, it would appear, was just determined to have something new wrong with him all the time. It was clearly a mental disorder. And Mrs. Henson seemed to want to live with her doom and gloom thoughts that she was dying every day. I would need a new plan. But what?

Mrs. Shay burst into my office and startled me from my thoughts.

"Doctor O'Hara, we are worried about Mrs. Walters."

"Why, what has happened? There is never anything wrong with Mrs. Walters."

"Nobody has seen her since yesterday. Mrs. Walters never misses a meal and she will not answer her door."

"It's locked?"

"Yes."

"Well, have security get the key and meet me at her room. We will have to go in and check on her."

"Yes, Doctor."

Mrs. Shay ran down the hall and I packed a few things into my little black bag. I made my way quickly to the door of Mrs. Walter's room, and was soon joined by Mrs. Shay and the security officer with the key. I decided to try knocking again first, before we entered.

"Hello? Mrs. Walters? Are you there? This is Doctor O'Hara. Hello?"

When we received no response, I nodded to the other man to open the door. I entered directly behind the officer and my heart sunk as my worst fear was realized. Mrs. Walters was lying face down on the floor. I rushed to her side and checked her pulse, but unfortunately she was dead. A heart attack was my initial guess.

"Umm, what the hell is all this?" the security officer

asked.

When Mrs. Shay gasped, I stood and took a look around. I was shocked to find the room full of small dolls. But these were not just ordinary dolls. These dolls resembled many of the folk that lived in Fairbrooke. So much so, that they were readily identifiable. Their likenesses were uncanny.

I picked up a doll that was the spitting image of Mister Briar, only to find that an elastic band was tied tightly around his throat. Then I spotted the doll of Mister Seagal. His left hand had been flattened by a hammer that rested nearby. A rock was placed on the chest of Mrs. Henson's doll. My mind reeled at this discovery. I looked around further and found the doll of Mrs. Ruttle, sitting in the sink, with water dripping onto the doll's head.

Voodoo dolls? The quiet and sweet Mrs. Walters was making voodoo dolls? How could I ever enter this into my records? An uncompleted doll sat on an end table next to her rocking chair. It's face resembled mine.

THE WOMAN ON THE BEACH

My first day of the boring conference was finally over. Listening to endless lectures, and watching horrendous slideshows with graphs and flowcharts, certainly takes its toll on one's mind. My brain checked out somewhere after our lunch break and I am not sure if I could recall a single word said after that point.

Fortunately, for me, I was staying in the same hotel as the conference, so I did not have far to travel to get back to my room. I could not complain one bit about the accommodations. From my window, I had a perfect unobstructed view of the beach and the boardwalk. My only problem was that it got dark fairly early this time of year, and by the time the conference was over, I did not have much daylight left to enjoy the quaint scenery.

I changed into something more comfortable and decided to get out for some fresh air. I thought a nice walk would do me some good and help clear my mind before the sun vanished.

The boardwalk here seemed to stretch on for miles. I passed many small restaurants and vendors selling food, and while each one smelled amazingly delicious, I was regrettably not very hungry. I had snacked on too many pastries all day at the conference and it ruined my appetite for dinner. But it was good to know that many options existed if I were to grow peckish later that evening.

I loved watching the waves roll onto the sand. There was something about the sound of it that could just wash away the troubles of the day. I could just stand there with my eyes closed and listen to that for hours.

I had walked nearly an hour in one direction and the sun was beginning to rapidly set. I reckoned it was best to head back to the hotel before it got too dark. I was unsure of just how I would pass the rest of the evening. Were I at home, I would be listening to radio programs, but my hotel room lacked a radio. It seemed as though I would miss my favorite program tonight, Jungle Johnny, unless the lounge area at the hotel had a radio. I picked up the pace as I considered that a strong possibility.

Last week's episode ended with Jungle Johnny surrounded by a group of angry apes. The rest of his crew had already left to return to their ship, so I had no idea how Johnny was going to escape this harrowing situation. The thought of missing this week's episode was enormously distressing.

As the lights of the hotel came into view, an odd sound from the beach caught my attention. Amid the crash of the waves, I thought I heard someone sobbing. I paused for a moment, attempting to shut out everything else and focus on that strange sound. I heard it again, and it was definitely someone upset, and a woman, I was certain of it.

I left the boardwalk for the sand of the beach and followed the sobbing through the darkness.

"Hello? Hello? Is everything alright?" I called out.

I received no response, but then suddenly leaped aside to avoid stumbling into a woman, who was sitting in the sand nearly ten feet from the water's edge.

"Oh, pardon me, I didn't see you sitting there," I apologized. "Miss, are you okay? I heard you sobbing from over on the boardwalk."

"I doubt that I will ever be okay again," the woman answered in a soft voice.

"Why would you say such a thing? Are you hurt?"

"My heart is hurt and I fear it shall never mend. Not until Donald returns."

"Donald? Who is Donald, if I may ask?"

"Donald is my husband."

"Donald is away? Traveling, perhaps?"

"He left on a fishing boat. He fishes for a living. I am waiting here for his return."

"Ah, I see. How long is he usually gone for?"

"A few days. A week at the most."

"Well, has it been a week yet? I am sure he will be back soon."

"He has been gone for three years now."

I wasn't quite sure if I had heard her properly. I thought she may have said three years.

"I am sorry, did you say three years?"

"Yes, three years," her sobbing renewed.

Now I understood her distress.

"Oh…ahh…I am sorry to hear that," I wasn't sure

what I could possibly say in response to that. "You believe he is coming back?"

"He will come back. He would never leave me. He loved me dearly."

"Then I am sure that he will too. I bid you a goodnight, miss, I must be returning to the hotel now. I mustn't miss Jungle Johnny if it can be avoided."

"Goodnight to you, sir."

With that, I took my leave and hurried back to the hotel with great haste. I navigated my way to the hotel lounge but was horrendously disappointed to learn that their radio had not been working. There would be no Jungle Johnny this evening. Wearing a long face, I returned to my room and decided to order some room service.

I changed into something more suitable for lying about in bed, and once I had devoured my cheesesteak sandwich, my mind drifted back to that poor woman on the beach. She was obviously not in her right mind. A man gone for three years was not going to be showing up on shore anytime soon. I could not be sure of their marital situation, but he had either decided not to return, or something unfortunate had befallen him. I chose to believe the latter. It was not uncommon for ships to go missing at sea. Victims of some terrible storm or something unforeseen had caused the ship to sink.

I could relate, somewhat, as to how that woman felt. I had lost my wife to the disease, six years past. It had been one terribly awful ordeal but at least I had had some closure. For better or worse, I was aware of my wife's fate. I could not imagine what it would be like to not know. To always wonder what happened to them. Were they alive? Were they dead? It broke my heart to think of that woman sitting on the beach, hoping that her husband would sail back at any moment.

Once my eyes had adjusted to the gloom on the beach, I had noticed that the woman was roughly the same age as I. Mid-to-late forties, I would guess. She was quite attractive with long dark hair. Her eyes were brown, I believed, with a lovely shape to them. She intrigued me and occupied most of my thoughts, before I drifted off to sleep that first night.

The second day of the conference was long and seemed to have dragged on endlessly. I was famished by the time we were let out and this time I did accompany some of the others to a nearby restaurant for dinner. I had a delicious lobster bisque, socialized for a spell, and then decided to call it a night.

After washing up and changing back at my room, I felt like a little fresh air before getting into bed. I stepped outside the hotel and closed my eyes, listening to the waves as I had done the previous night.

My eyes shot open as I heard a familiar sobbing sound. Good heavens, that woman must have been sitting on the beach again. I followed the sound and found the same woman sitting in the same general area.

"Pardon the intrusion, miss, but I couldn't help but hear you again as I stepped out for a bit of air. You may recall me from last night."

"I do, and I am sorry to have disturbed you."

"No, no, you did not disturb me at all. May I sit?"

"You may, although I don't make for great company."

Not caring about getting sand in my trousers, I took a seat on the beach next to the woman. We were facing the ocean, though, at this time of night there was nothing to see. Of course the sound of the waves was indeed soothing.

"I am Albert," I said. "May I have the pleasure of your name?"

"My name is Anna."

"A lovely name. Tell me, Anna, are you out here often? Waiting, like this?"

"Every day."

"Every day? For three years?"

"Yes. Every day."

The poor, poor girl. I truly felt for her.

"Have you ever considered why Donald may have been gone this long? An accident, perhaps?"

"There was a terrible storm the night he and the others had left. Some of the locals say the storm took them but I don't believe that."

"Well, if I may ask, what do you think happened, then? I don't want to appear pessimistic, but three years is a long time, and the timing of that storm is a tragic coincidence."

"Maybe their ship did get damaged and it made getting home more difficult. There are a lot of islands out there, they could have been stranded on one. Someone could find them any day now."

I could understand her not wishing to think of the worst scenario but three years was a long time to try to fool one's self. I decided to change the subject.

"You must live in town, do you?"

"Yes, we have a small house just five minutes from the beach here. Are you a tourist?"

"Well, I am here for a conference. It's rather boring,

to be honest, but sometimes it is nice to get away. I am from the Big City and don't often get to enjoy the sights and sounds of the ocean."

"Ah, a Big City boy. What do you do there?"

"Please don't hate me if I tell you, but I sell insurance."

"Nothing wrong with that."

"I am here for a dull sales conference and it takes considerable effort to remain awake in there all day. I really don't know how I manage it. And what about yourself? What is it that you do, well, when you aren't here at the beach?"

"I spend most of my time here. I want to make sure I am the first one that Donald sees when he gets back."

"You know, Anna, I know how you feel. I, too, have lost someone. The grief is terrible and it does take a long time to get over. I understand that people all deal with it in different ways."

"Was it your wife?"

I then proceeded to tell Anna about my wife and what happened all those years ago. She listened intently and we shared more than a few tears. We talked for hours until I really had to get some sleep. She remained at the beach, staring out into the blackness of the sea, waiting.

The following day dragged on dreadfully. All I could think about was Anna and how I wanted to join her at the beach and talk some more. Watching the clock only seemed to make the time pass more slowly. Regrettably, the sun had already set by the time I was released from my daytime prison, and I thought I would forego any plans for dinner and head straight to the beach. In short order, I found Anna, sobbing as usual.

This night, I changed up the topics and steered clear of dead loved ones and missing husbands. I got Anna to smile and even laugh. She had a stunning smile and it felt marvelous to be able to cheer her up. She clearly did not have anyone else in her life to provide that for her.

"I really appreciate these talks, Albert. It has been a pleasant distraction. When do you leave?"

"Friday is the last day of my conference," I said with a sigh. "And I have really enjoyed these talks as well. I believe the sun will be coming up soon and I should try to sleep for an hour or two at least. Shall I join you again, when the conference is done for the day?"

"Yes, of course, I would like that."

I was unable to sleep for even a minute when I got back to my room. My every thought was of Anna and of that smile of hers. As per usual, I attended the next day of the conference in body only, as my mind was elsewhere. We even broke into groups for a project and I was utterly useless. I stared blankly out the window, wondering what Anna was doing at that very moment.

When the conference finally concluded for the day, I dashed toward my room to get changed. I was intercepted by one of the employees who worked for the hotel.

"Ah, pardon me, sir, I have some good news."

"Oh?"

"Yes, we have fixed the problem with our radio and they are doing a rebroadcast of the Jungle Johnny episode you had missed from the other night. It will be at seven this evening."

"Oh, ah, yes, that is fantastic. Thank you for the news."

As I was changing, I considered this news but found

that I had no interest in Jungle Johnny this night. I had not even given Johnny a second thought since I had gotten to know Anna. I still didn't know whether Johnny escaped the angry apes, and for the moment, that was not a priority to me. I wanted nothing more than to spend every free moment with the woman on the beach.

I had room service deliver two ham and cheese sandwiches and promptly headed to the beach. It was quite dark again and I cursed the conference and its long hours. I located Anna, who was again sobbing, although her face did brighten this time at my arrival. Ah, that smile.

I offered her my second sandwich but she said she had already eaten. I hadn't realized how famished I was, until I finished both sandwiches in record time. We then spent many, many hours, talking as we had done the previous nights. We talked about family and friends and just life in general. I learned that she loved to garden and that she felt awful for neglecting hers these last few years. We even laughed some more and she seemed in better spirits.

"Anna, tomorrow is the last day of the conference. Would it be alright if I asked you to dinner? Some of the other folk have been raving about this seafood place just down the boardwalk. You are probably familiar with it but I would love for you to join me."

Her smile faded. "I would enjoy that, Albert, but Donald could be back any time now and I should be here."

"Anna, it has been three years. We could just be an hour and then come right back here."

"I am sorry, I had better not. Just in case."

I sighed. "Ok, well, how about I get some take out

and we will just have our dinner here at the beach? How does that work?"

"That works, I would like that," she nodded.

We spoke for a while longer, before I really did need to try and sleep. I had been attempting to function on little to no sleep this week and it was beginning to catch up to me. I fell asleep with Anna on my mind and she was the first thing that entered into my thoughts when I awoke.

An idea struck me that morning and I ran to use the telephone in the hotel lobby. I made arrangements to extend my trip until the end of the weekend and paid out of my own pocket to keep my room for another two days. I was hoping Anna would be as excited as I was. I felt we had made a genuine connection. I thought maybe if I spent the weekend at the beach with her, I could even manage to get her away for a short time. To show her that there was still a life to be lived away from the beach. After three years, she needed to understand that Donald was not coming back.

To my absolute joy, the conference ended early that Friday. It was only noon when they bid us farewell. I had not yet had the pleasure of really enjoying the view of the beach during the daylight hours, and of course the best part was that I now had more time to spend with Anna.

So excited was I, that I did not even bother to change. I made my way down to the beach in my jacket and tie, in search of this woman that I had come to…love? Yes, love, I could admit it. She had an extraordinary personality and every moment we spent talking was a delight.

With the sun high in the sky, I was finally afforded a perfect view of the beach. There were several people lying in the sand this day but Anna was not among them. I searched up and down the area where she always sat, without an ounce of luck. I even called out her name. I supposed she might not have come yet, after all, the woman needed her sleep as well.

I was about to approach a couple and ask if they might have seen Anna, when something strange caught my eye. I walked over to a spot on the beach to inspect what appeared to be some kind of memorial. A wooden cross was stuck into the sand and various types of flowers had been laid all around it. When I knelt down, I could see something written on the cross. It read, "Anna Hallworth. Forever Waiting."

I stood, utterly confused. Looking to the boardwalk, I spotted the hotel employee who had relayed to me the good news about the repaired radio.

"Hello? You there, hello?"

He stopped and I joined him on the boardwalk.

"Hello again, sir, what may I do for you?"

"That cross over there on the beach, what can you tell me about it?"

"That is a sad tale, to be sure."

"It says Anna Hallworth on it. Forever Waiting. What does that mean?"

"They say that Anna Hallworth died from a broken heart. She used to sit there, every day, waiting for her husband to return. He had gone out on a fishing vessel and a wicked storm capsized the ship and killed all on board. They say Anna could never accept that news and sat there every day, believing he would still come home to her."

"She died? When did she die?" my heart skipped a

beat.

"Oh, about fifteen years ago. Some people say at night, if you listen very carefully, you can still hear her sobbing."

MISTY MCDONNELL AND THE EXPERIMENTAL TREATMENT

The doctor was wearing his serious face today and Misty knew that was not good. She guessed that in his mind, he was wearing his poker face, which would be impossible to read. But when the usually jovial doctor was not smiling, that gave it all away.

"I am afraid I don't have good news, Misty. I am sorry."

Misty sighed. It was not like it wasn't expected anyway. "How long do I have?"

The doctor fidgeted with a pen and found it difficult to look the older woman in the eyes. He hated this part of his job the most. "A month. Maybe two, if I had to guess."

"Well, it's not really a surprise, is it?"

"Misty, I am sorry, we have tried everything. I just

99

wish we..."

"It's alright," she cut him off. "I understand. I know you have done all that you could. That's just life. And I am old."

Misty McDonnell was eighty-six years old. She felt fortunate that her sight and hearing had stuck with her for all these years but the disease had finally claimed her. She had spent the last six months of her life bed-ridden and requiring aid for even the smallest of tasks. The Fairbrooke senior's home in the upper-east side of the Big City is where she now called home. There were certainly worse places that one could live but she disliked it here all the same. She viewed it as just a place where people came to die. Almost everyone around her complained of phantom aches and pains. They were all positive the end was near, though, the doctors never found anything wrong with them. Misty only wished she had phantom problems; hers were all too real.

Later that evening, after receiving her most terrible news, the other reason she hated living in this home walked into her room.

"I hear you won't be with us for very much longer. It's about time," said the male nurse.

Misty frowned. "I thought you didn't work on Saturdays, Kevin."

"I don't, it's Friday. Your old brain has stopped working again. Want me to give it a shake?"

"Friday?" Misty looked up to the clock on the wall. "Oh, I almost forgot. Quick, turn on the radio. It's almost time for Detective Darke."

Since the disease had stolen the strength from her body and she could no longer walk, the only enjoyment

Misty got was from her radio programs. Detective Darke was her absolute favorite. He was such a clever detective and each week he had to solve the most bizarre crimes. It saddened her to think that soon she would not be able follow the exploits of Detective Darke and the wild adventures of Jungle Johnny.

"I am afraid the radio doesn't work."

"Don't be absurd. It was working just fine yesterday."

"That was yesterday. Today it's not working."

"You never even tried it."

"There was a note from another staff member. Said it wasn't working."

Misty was not a hateful person but she hated Kevin. He was a miserable wretch who took great joy in tormenting her, and the other seniors, she imagined. She was fearful of mentioning it to anyone else in case it just made the situation worse. Kevin had even said as much on several occasions. Many of the other nurses were quite rude as well but Kevin was the worst of them all.

"What's for dinner? I am hungry," Misty asked, after giving up on pressing the issue of the radio.

"Here, have some crackers."

Kevin threw a small package of crackers at the older woman before leaving the room. Fortunately, the crackers did land on top of her, within reach. She fumed inside, knowing that Detective Darke was about to start and that horrible man refused to turn the radio on for her. For a moment, she even considered crawling to the radio and turning it on herself, but quickly dismissed that notion. The program would probably be over by the time she made it that far. And it was no use ringing the bell for assistance since Kevin would be the only one to respond.

Misty sighed and ate her crackers, then attempted to get some sleep.

Days later, when Kevin was off work, one of the other nurses turned on the radio. Of course, there was nothing wrong with it and it worked just fine. That just made Misty all the more angrier. But at least she was able to listen to the Jungle Johnny program that evening. It was a thrilling episode with its usual cliff-hanger ending that left the listeners craving to know what would happen next. Johnny was alone in the jungle and surrounded by savage apes. How could he possibly escape this time, she wondered.

Sadness overcame Misty once again. She did not have any family left alive and her friends were few, but she counted Jungle Johnny and Detective Darke as part of her family. Life inside Fairbrooke was not great, but she so thoroughly enjoyed her radio programs that she found she was most distressed about leaving this world and never hearing them again. The joy those shows brought her, outweighed her loneliness.

The next few weeks that passed with Kevin on duty were miserable. Misty learned a valuable trick, though, she had the morning nurse leave the radio on all day and then Kevin could not claim it was broken when he came in. That did not prevent him from tormenting her in other ways but at least she did not miss her programs.

One somber afternoon, Doctor Whethers paid Misty a visit. He had not seen her since delivering her the bad news.

"How are we holding up?" he asked.

"This waiting to die is horrible," she replied.

"I can only imagine. Aside from that, how are you

feeling?"

"Weak. Just very weak."

"No pain?"

"Not yet, no."

"That's good, then."

"Doctor, I am not ready to die. My life has become miserable but the thought of being without Detective Darke and Jungle Johnny pains me the most. I so enjoy listening to those programs. I don't have any family left but I feel as though they are my family."

"I apologize if this question sounds a tad inappropriate, but do you have much money in savings?"

"Well, I do have a tidy sum left but I have not yet written a will. I know I can't take the money with me but I haven't yet decided what to do with it. Why do you ask?"

"I was just curious. I was reading something the other day that perhaps you might find interesting."

"Oh?"

The doctor closed the door to her room and pulled a chair up next to her bed. Misty had been fortunate to get her own room and have the privacy it afforded. She could not imagine what the doctor had to say, while exercising such caution. He even lowered his voice as he explained.

"A colleague of mine had suggested I read something quite recently. This is not widely known, as it is being kept only within certain circles."

"Yes?" Misty sat up, fully intrigued.

"Well, in Eastern Europe, apparently, a small group of doctors have been working on an experimental treatment for the disease. For many terminal ailments, actually."

"Experimental treatment? To what end?"

"From what I have read, they can prolong life and improve upon the quality of life. They claim to have achieved success so far with a few patients."

"Are you saying they have found a cure for the disease?"

"Something like that. They are not calling it a cure, just yet, but essentially it would be the same thing."

"Are they bringing this treatment here? Will it be available in the Big City?"

"I am afraid not. They are closely guarding their techniques. They are quite secretive about the details but boast success with it. They also charge a large sum to those seeking this treatment."

"So, it is of little use to me here, then."

"Well, not quite so. That is why I inquired about your financial situation. As you said, you cannot take the money with you after...well, after everything. And if you have no family you wish to leave the money with, then it may be possible to take a gamble."

"A gamble?"

"Yes. If you have nothing to left to lose, and you possess the necessary funds, you could utilize that money for the flight over there and the treatment. I say gamble because I have not seen the results of this treatment, firsthand, so I cannot say whether it really works or not. I can only go by what I have read, though, the source is reliable."

"How much would this be?"

"It's a lot. How about I write the sum down for you, along with a phone number and other contact information, and just leave it here on your nightstand. Look it over and give it some thought. I wish I could have been more help to you, Misty, I am sorry."

The doctor scribbled down the information he promised and left the piece of paper on the nightstand, within reach. He smiled at Misty and left her alone. She spent the next few hours mulling over the doctor's words before picking up the piece of paper. It was a considerable amount they were asking but could you really put a price on life? Misty would not have been so keen to extend her bed-ridden life but they were claiming to improve the quality of life and not just prolong it. Perhaps it would be possible to live on her own again and leave Fairbrooke. As hefty a fee as it was, Misty did have enough money saved to cover the cost of the treatment and a flight, with some left over. There would not be much left but she was sure she could manage something if the treatment was successful. If it was not successful, then it would not really matter to her anyway.

The following day, it was as though Misty was not present at all. Nurses came and went and she paid them little heed, so lost in thought was she. It was not until much later, that she noticed she had been oblivious to the radio and missed the Ollie Organ show. Ollie was a brilliant accordion player and always brought on fantastic musical guests. As Misty awoke from her deep thoughts, she caught Ollie Organ just as he was signing off for the evening.

She looked to the clock and could not believe she had spent the entire day inside her mind, working out all the pros and cons of this possible treatment. She was not even sure what the treatment entailed. Would it be painful? Was it a lengthy procedure? Had there been many failures thus far? So many questions swirled about her head.

Misty had made up her mind during Kevin's next shift. He had brought her soup for her dinner and purposely spilled it all over her and left her like that for the rest of the evening. She figured she was dying anyway, so why not take the trip, regardless. If the treatment failed, then at least she would have escaped Kevin and could die someplace else with some relative peace. Surely, that alone was worth every cent of the costly endeavor.

In the morning, Misty asked one of the more pleasant nurses to bring her to one of the sitting rooms so she could look out the window. She strategically requested her wheelchair to be placed within reach of the phone in that room. Once the nurse had left, and once she was sure that the few other folk in the room were preoccupied with conversation, she picked up the phone and dialed the number the doctor had left her.

A kind man answered her call and was pleased to hear from her. He had a thick Eastern European accent but spoke English very well. Misty explained her situation and how she had obtained the number. The man, who identified himself as Victor, was quite helpful and related to her all the steps that would be required, were she to proceed seriously with this treatment. She attempted to get details of the treatment, itself, without much luck. Victor was vague when it came to the procedure but assured her that it had been perfected and would be successful. He guaranteed her an immense improvement on the quality of her life and the disease would hinder her no more.

The man suggested she take some time to give it further thought but Misty's mind was made. She informed him that more time was unnecessary and she was ready to proceed with whatever needed to be done. A second phone call was required the next day, as Misty had to get her banking information in order. The considerable fee for the treatment included the flight and chauffeur service from Fairbrooke.

Victor requested that the full amount of the cost be wired to him before any plans could be made. Misty was hesitant at first, wondering if this was some scheme to swindle seniors out of money, but went ahead with it anyway. She reminded herself that she was dying so nothing really mattered. The disease would claim her whether she had money left in the bank or not.

Two long days went by, as Misty waited impatiently to hear any news from Victor. At least she found a pleasant distraction with Detective Darke on the radio, well, that is until Kevin arrived and unplugged it.

"What do you think you are doing? I was listening to that."

"Sorry, too many complaints about the noise."

"The noise? It wasn't loud at all. And besides, Mrs. Heinrichs and Mrs. Florence can't even hear."

"Yeah, well, too many complaints. Nothing I can do about it."

"You plug that in right…"

"Ah, hello? Ms. McDonnell?"

Their conversation was interrupted by the arrival of two men dressed in dark suits.

"Visiting hours are over," Kevin stated.

"Yes, I am Ms. McDonnell," Misty replied, ignoring Kevin. "Who are you both?"

"We work for Victor. It is time, Ms. McDonnell."

"Time? As in right now?"

"Yes. We can gather up any belongings you would

like to take. Your flight leaves in two hours and we will be transporting you to the airport."

"Leaving? What is this nonsense?" Kevin demanded to know. "You know you are not allowed to go anywhere at this time. You have not gotten any approvals from the office staff."

"Kevin, go to hell," Misty smiled ear to ear; that felt wonderful.

"We will see about this," he said, storming out of the room.

"Pay him no mind. I don't own much. Just a handful of clothes from the closet over there and a few knick-knacks from my drawer. I wasn't expecting things to move so quickly."

"Your money transfer went through so Victor did not want to waste any time. We were told to retrieve you. Is this an inconvenient time?"

"No, no, not at all. Time is something I don't have a lot of, so the quicker the better."

Butterflies danced about in Misty's stomach as she watched the two men pack up her meager belongings into two small suitcases she had stored away. It was happening so fast but it was for the better, she kept reminding herself.

They avoided Kevin and the other staff as Misty was wheeled out to a waiting limousine. She had never been in such a fancy car in her entire life. The two men were very gentle and patient as they helped her get inside. It was not until Fairbrooke was far behind them, that Misty thought she should have left a note for Doctor Whethers. A thank-you letter or at least a good-bye. She could very well die at her appointed destination and nobody would ever know where she had gone. Oh well, she thought, she had bigger concerns now.

Then it dawned on her that she did not even know where she was going. "Pardon me, gentlemen, but where is it exactly that I will be going to?"

"Far from here," one of them answered.

"Yes, but where exactly? Victor was never clear about that."

"Eastern Europe."

"I figured that. Whereabouts?"

"We honestly don't know, ma'am. We just take you to the airport."

Misty remained quiet the rest of the way, just enjoying the drive and getting what could very well be her last look at the Big City. She was quite surprised that the limo brought her straight to a runway with a small private plane.

"Wow, my own private plane?"

"All part of the fee you paid."

The two men helped get her settled onto the plane and introduced her to the captain and a woman who would see to her needs during the flight. They wished her a safe trip and the plane was in the air in no time at all. Misty tried to elicit more information out of the female crewmember but she was as much in the dark about everything as the other two men. She knew nothing else about what was going on except to make Misty comfortable during the fifteen-hour flight.

Misty hoped she could just sleep most of the way but sleep would not come to her. Her mind was working on overdrive as the reality of this bizarre situation was kicking in. She did not know where she was going. She did not know the people she would be meeting. She would be undergoing some secret experimental treatment to rid herself of her disease. She had every right to be terrified and the closer they got to their destination, that immense feeling of nervousness grew tenfold.

The flight passed without incident and she was soon sitting in the back of a small car. The driver was an extremely pale young man who appeared emaciated. She wondered if he had the disease as well but withheld her questions as he was not the friendliest of fellows. He spoke not a word and focused solely on the winding road ahead of him.

He would not even tell her what country it was that she had landed in. The landscape was beautiful, though, wherever she was. Forests of tall green trees. Distant mountains in every direction she turned. She did her best to focus on the scenery and think less about her creepy escort. It was best for her not to second-guess her decision as it was far too late for that now. Her body was getting weaker by the day and the sand in her hourglass would soon run out.

With the combination of the long flight, her weakening body, and the jostling of the car, sleep finally claimed Misty. When her eyes had finally reopened, it was dark outside and the car pulled into a long, gated-driveway, which ended in front of a magnificent-looking mansion. It was all made of stone and had the feel of a castle, only on a smaller scale. Green ivy creeped its way all over the house, threatening to engulf it entirely.

Misty's initial thought was that this looked nothing like a hospital, or a senior's home, for that matter.

"Driver, are you sure you have the right place? I am here in search of a medical procedure."

The driver said nothing and exited the car, retrieving

Misty's suitcases from the trunk. Another man, as equally pale and as equally unnerving, came and helped Misty out of the car and into her wheelchair. Without a word, that man brought her to the beautifully-carved, wooden front door. Two stone gargoyles clung to the wall on each side of the door, leering down at her.

She was about to ask the strange man if they would need to knock, when the door opened. Out stepped a tall and gaunt middle-aged man. His salt and pepper hair was combed perfectly back and his pale complexion matched that of the other two men. He was very well-dressed and obviously wealthy.

"Misty McDonnell, it is a pleasure to finally make your acquaintance," he said in a familiar voice. "I am Victor. I trust that your journey was uneventful?"

"Yes, yes, it was fine, if not a touch too long."

"Yes, it is quite a distance from the Big City to here."

"Where is here?"

"Why don't we bring you inside, away from this chill night air. I am sure you have many questions and we can begin your treatment straightaway."

"Do you really think you can cure me of the disease?"

"My dear, I guarantee it."

*   *   *   *

The sound of a radio from down the hall grabbed Kevin's attention. Further investigation revealed that it was coming from Misty McDonnell's old room. Curious, Kevin entered the room and gasped.

"What are you doing here? I thought you left? How did you get back in here?"

Misty lay in her bed, buddled up with a thick blanket, while listening to Detective Darke on the radio. It was a particularly interesting episode and she grew upset that Kevin had interrupted. She mouthed a reply but no words came out. She appeared paler than he had previously remembered.

"What are you saying? I can't hear you. Explain yourself, you old witch."

Again, she attempted to answer but it only came out as a faint whisper. Frustrated, Kevin stood beside her bed and leaned over.

"What are you trying to say?"

Misty smiled and spoke in a perfectly calm voice. "I said, shut up. You are interrupting Detective Darke."

"What did you just say?" Kevin roared. "You miserable old….GACK!"

Misty rose from her bed and grabbed Kevin by the throat, cutting off his sentence. His eyes bulged from his head in shock. Misty stood and held Kevin off the floor with one hand, then threw him against the wall with such force, that he nearly crashed straight through.

Before he could even think to cry out for help, Misty hoisted him from the floor as if he weighed nothing at all. She smiled at him, revealing razor-sharp fangs, and then sunk those fangs deep into Kevin's throat. Misty drank his body clean of blood and then cast it aside.

She sat on the edge of her bed until Detective Darke had solved this week's murder. With the program over, Misty exited through the room's window and never returned to Fairbrooke again.

SNAKE OIL

It was an oppressively hot afternoon and Sheriff Ward sat outside his office, fanning himself in a poor attempt to cool off. He had made a tactical retreat from the office, as he had found it hotter inside than it was out. The main thoroughfare was nearly devoid of townsfolk this day and the Sheriff chalked it up to the heat. It was normally hot this time of year but today was extremely so. At least the heat kept most people indoors, out of the sun, and not out and about causing trouble. It would be a lazy day, or so he thought.

"Sheriff! Sheriff!" a familiar voice shouted from down the road.

Sheriff Ward turned to regard Doctor Tuttle shuffling his way through the dusty street. He leaped to his feet, as the old doctor rarely moved that fast unless there was an emergency.

"What is it, Doc? Someone hurt?" he asked, after

meeting the other man in the middle of the thoroughfare.

The doctor motioned for him to wait a moment while he caught his breath.

"Well, spit it out, Doc. What happened?"

"A stranger in town…"

"Yes, and?"

"He is out past Miller's Grocery Store…"

"Alright, yes, and what has he done? Come on, Doc."

"Well…he…he is out there peddling snake oil."

The Sheriff relaxed and shook his head. "Snake oil? You come running down the street like the devil is behind you because some stranger is selling snake oil? Gosh darnit, Doc! I thought someone got shot or robbed."

"Well, they are being robbed. A mob of folk are over there right now buying up all that rubbish."

"If someone is not holding a gun to their fool heads to make them buy it, then no, Doc, they ain't being robbed, they are just plum stupid."

"It is illegal all the same! He is claiming his tonics can heal all sorts of ailments."

"Yeah, it's still fraud."

"What are you going to do about it? Huh?"

"Now, you just simmer down. I'll head over there and take a look-see for myself."

"I am sorry I have to take you away from your nap over there in front of your office."

"I wasn't napping. And you better get yourself out of the sun before you keel over dead and we need to find ourselves a new doctor."

The usually grumpy doctor mumbled something under his breath and shuffled into the closest saloon to get some shade and possibly a drink, since he was there.

Sheriff Ward elected to walk and made the fifteen minute trek out to Miller's Grocery Store. Sure enough, he spotted a large crowd gathered around a wagon in a pasture, just out behind the store. So, it wasn't the heat after all that made the town appear to be dead. Most folk were here, listening to the sales pitch of the tall, white-haired stranger.

The man stood on a stool at the back of his large, enclosed, weather-beaten wagon. On the side of the wagon, written in red paint, was "ALL ELIXIRS – ONE DOLLAR." The back doors were wide open, with many cases of a bottled liquid visible within. The magical elixir. The stranger held a bottle in each hand and addressed the crowd like a carnival barker.

"That's right, folks, it's only one dollar to cure any ailment. I have an elixir for everything. Have a bad back? Sore neck? Trouble walking? You tell me what's wrong and I will fetch the bottle that will fix it."

The Sheriff watched old Andy Anderson hobble his way to the front. Andy owned a farm on the outskirts of town and was thrown from a horse many years ago. He had broken his leg in the fall and it had never healed properly.

"My leg is in constant pain," he told the stranger. "I don't get around as well as I used to."

"Leg pain, you say? Have trouble walking? I have just the thing for you."

The stranger rummaged through the back of the wagon until he produced the bottle that he was looking for. The Sheriff thought the bottle looked exactly like all the rest.

"Here you go, my friend. This elixir is specifically for leg pain. Drink three mouthfuls a day until the bottle is empty and your leg pain will be gone. Why, you will be running around in no time. That'll be one dollar."

Sheriff Ward smirked. He guessed that three mouthfuls a day would take about a week before the bottle was empty. Snake oil salesmen never promised instant results. They needed to get as far away from town as possible before the unfortunate individual realized they had been taken for a fool. In a week's time, this stranger would be clear across the territory, peddling his wares to another group of ignorant folk.

"Alright, who's next? Who needs a cure? Ok, you sir, what exactly is bothering…oh, hello, Sheriff, a pleasure to make your acquaintance."

"Okay, everyone, go on about your business. Show's over. Go on now, get!"

"But, Sheriff, you know how bad my back gets around this time of year, you know that. I was gonna purchase one of these here bottles."

"Not today, you won't. Go on home, Teddy. I know you still owe Mr. Oswald three dollars so it seems to me that you could make better use of the dollar you were about to give this charlatan."

The stranger pressed a hand against his heart. "Charlatan? Now, Sheriff, you wound me. I am here only to help these good folk."

"And you are gonna help them by closing up that wagon of yours. What's your name, stranger?"

"Gabriel."

"Gabriel, what?"

"Why, I never thought to give myself a last name. I just go by Gabriel."

"Where are you from?"

"Far from here."

"Look, I wouldn't keep cracking wise if I were you, I ain't in a good mood today."

"I wasn't causing any trouble. I told you, all I was doing was trying to help these people."

"The folk around here don't have a lot of money. They are decent hard-working folk that can't afford to just go throwing away a whole dollar."

"It's not throwing it away when they are cured of their aches and pains."

"You and I both know your snake oil ain't gonna heal anyone of any aches or pains."

"Snake oil? You insult me again. Why, I will have you know I have been curing folk all over this glorious country."

"How long were you planning on staying here in town?"

"Well, not long. I have to be on my way tomorrow morning. Lotsa sick people need seeing to."

"I am gonna invite you to stay with us for a week."

"A week? Sheriff, I am afraid I really need to be on my way tomorrow."

"I insist."

"Am I under arrest or something?"

"Not yet, you ain't."

"A whole week?"

"Yup. You are gonna hang around here until all those people you sold your elixirs to are finished drinking those bottles. Should be pretty satisfying for you to see all those happy faces from all those cured people. Right?"

"Well, of course it would be but I have to be elsewhere. A week is a long time, Sheriff."

"You can stay at the hotel just over yonder. Their rates are quite reasonable and I imagine that won't be a problem with all the sales you made today already."

"I don't sell my elixirs for profit, I will have you know. The money just covers my expenses and keeps my old mule here fed. I sell these for the pure joy of helping those in need."

"And that's another thing. You won't be selling another bottle for the rest of your stay. Got it?"

"But, Sheriff!"

"Don't you but Sheriff me. No more peddling your snake oil. You hear me? Or you can spend your week in a jail cell instead of the hotel."

The man grumbled while he began packing up his wagon.

"And don't think about skipping town. I am gonna have eyes on you. One week and then you can go."

"Fine."

Sheriff Ward waited around until Gabriel finished packing up and then watched him make his way over to the hotel, tethering his mule just outside. Satisfied that the stranger wasn't going anywhere, anytime soon, the Sheriff returned to his office and went through a pile of wanted posters. He was curious to see if Gabriel's face had decorated any of them. One came close, a wanted murderer from the northern territories, but the nose and eye color were not quite a match. Not enough to warrant suspicion, anyhow. Either way, the Sheriff would dispatch a few men to keep eyes on the stranger and prevent him from leaving town until a week's time had gone by.

The next few days passed lazily until Doc Tuttle burst into the Sheriff's office, startling him.

"I thought you were going to get rid of that snake oil salesman!" he said, in quite a perturbed tone. "Why is he still here in town? You should have either run him out or locked him up."

"Now, Doc, I just can't lock people up for no reason."

"You have a reason. He is a fraud and stealing money from the folk around here."

"Well, it just so happens that I have asked him to stick around for a week. I reckon that's just enough time for people to realize his elixirs don't work. Then I can call him a fraud with proof. But don't you worry, I have told him not to sell any more of those bottles."

"And a fine job of sheriffing you seem to be doing. That weasel is over at Fanny's Saloon peddling his wares again. Got a line going straight out the door, he has."

"What?"

"Go and see for yourself, if your naptime is over. I saw Wilbur Harrison this morning and asked him why he hadn't come to see me about his headache pills. He told me he wouldn't need headache pills anymore. And would you like me to tell you why Wilbur Harrison doesn't think he needs his headache pills anymore?"

"You are gonna tell me anyway."

"Because Wilbur Harrison told me he got an elixir from over at Fanny's and it's gonna cure his headaches for good. That fraud is gonna have people giving up real medicine for his snake oil."

"Alright, alright, I am going over there right now."

"You see to it."

As much as Sheriff Ward wanted to rush over to Fanny's, he took his time, only to anger Doc Tuttle. His own anger level rose, however, when he spotted people lined up out the door of the saloon and onto the street, just as the Doc had described.

"Get out of here, all y'all," he shouted to everyone outside the saloon. "Don't go throwing your hard-earned money away on snake oil. Come on, now, I ain't kidding. Get."

Just then, a young woman came rushing out of the saloon holding a bottle of elixir.

"Madison?" the Sheriff looked at her, bewildered. "You are young and healthy, what are you doing with that bottle?"

"Well, Sheriff, you know my Ma can't see all too well. That nice man in there gave me an elixir that will bring her sight back."

He shook his head. "Is there no end to what you folk will believe?"

Sheriff Ward stormed into the saloon and began pushing people out of the way, shouting at them to go back home or to go back to work. He seethed with anger as he approached the stranger and grabbed the wrist shackles from his belt.

"You are under arrest, Gabriel," he declared.

"Arrest? Whatever for?"

"I told you days ago that you were not to peddle any more of that snake oil while you were in town. You were not to take any more money from these people."

"But, Sheriff, I wasn't selling any of my elixirs."

"Huh? I just caught you red-handed."

"No, I was not selling them. I was giving them away, for free."

"For free?"

"I told you, I am just here to help people and there are so many here in need."

The Sheriff called over Fanny, the saloon's owner. "Is he telling the truth? Did he take money from anyone?"

"No, he didn't, Sheriff. In fact, a few folk were insisting on paying him and he refused to even accept a cent."

"See? I haven't committed any crimes here. I didn't sell any, just like you told me."

"You get back to the hotel and take all this snake oil with you. I don't want you selling it and I don't want you giving any of it away. You are filling folk's heads with your fool ideas of being cured."

"But, Sheriff."

"No buts. This is your last warning."

For the next several days, Doc Tuttle was relentless and was a constant thorn in the Sheriff's side. He wanted Gabriel out of town, something fierce. Sheriff Ward was finally beginning to understand why. The folk in town were turning to the stranger to fix their various problems and were ignoring the Doc, altogether. Business had dropped for almost a week now. The doctor made money from visits and prescribing medicine. The Sheriff figured that Doc Tuttle dealt in a little bit of snake oil himself and now he had some competition.

The week was nearly up when the peace and quiet of one afternoon was interrupted by frantic shouting.

"Murder! Murder! Oh dear Lord, Murder!"

Sheriff Ward found Virginia Blake, sobbing in the street with folk beginning to gather around.

"Sheriff, there has been a murder!" she proclaimed, between sobs.

"Who was murdered, Virginia?"

"Clarence. Oh dear Lord, he murdered Clarence."

Clarence was Virginia's husband and had been bed-ridden and knocking on death's door for months. The Sheriff was surprised that Clarence had even lasted this long.

"Who murdered him, Virginia? How did it happen?"

"That stranger," she continued to weep. "I sought him out for his help and he poisoned my husband, Sheriff. He murdered poor Clarence."

"I saw the stranger in the hotel lobby just moments ago, Sheriff," a man said.

"Do you need any help?" another asked. "Need us to help you string him up?"

"Nobody is stringing anyone up, just yet. You men help Virginia here over to my office. I will see to the stranger."

As suggested, Gabriel was found sitting on a sofa in the hotel lobby, sipping some tea. Concern was written on his face as he looked up to regard the arrival of Sheriff Ward.

"Afternoon, Sheriff. Is there a problem?"

"Virginia Blake is accusing you of murder. She says you poisoned her husband."

"That is simply not true. That woman asked me if I had an elixir to help her husband."

"You were told not give anyone else that snake oil of yours," the Sheriff growled.

"She was so desperate for help, so I went with her. Have you seen her husband lately?"

"I have."

"Then you know how badly off he was. There was

nothing I could do to help. I did not have an elixir that could fix him but I did have one that could ease his suffering."

"So you admit you poisoned him?"

"No! I didn't say that. I gave him an elixir for the pain, that's all. He died all on his own."

"So, he drank some of your snake oil and then died, shortly thereafter."

"He would have died anyway. I merely took his pain away, as per his own request."

"You are under arrest. Come with me."

"I didn't murder that man! I helped him!"

"Let's go. You have some new accommodations."

A mob had now gathered around the Sheriff's office as he approached with his prisoner. Doc Tuttle was there and apparently had been prodding the group into a frenzy.

"Murderer!" they shouted. "Hang him!"

After Gabriel was securely locked away in a cell and Virginia was given a cup of tea and a place to sit and rest, Doc Tuttle pulled Sheriff Ward out the back door.

"I warned you about him. Now you have a murder on your hands."

"Doc, you and I both know that Clarence could have gone any day now."

"Nonsense. I had kept him alive this long with real medicine. He could have gotten better."

"I highly doubt that."

"It doesn't matter what you doubt, you have to look at the facts. That man gave Clarence a drink of his elixir and Clarence died right after. That was poisoning. That was murder."

Sheriff Ward could not deny those facts but it did not

make his job any easier. Gabriel continued to plead his innocence and that he was only here to help people. The Sheriff delayed any type of trial until the week had passed, hoping to gather further evidence. A day after the week's deadline he had given the stranger had come and gone, a mob, once again, gathered outside the office, shouting. Doc Tuttle, of course, was among them, but a few of the others surprised the Sheriff.

"Andy? You seem to be walking just fine. Mrs. Rosewood? You can see?"

"The pain in my leg is gone," Andy replied.

"I can see again," Madison's mother added.

"So, the elixirs worked? Why are you here, then?"

"Witchcraft!" shouted Doc Tuttle. "How long before these so-called healed folk just drop dead like poor Clarence did? Witchcraft, I tell ya!"

"I have been poisoned, Sheriff," said Rory Tate. "I don't have any ache or pain left in my body. It's gone completely numb from that poison, I just know it. I wanna see that man hang before I meet my end."

"Hang him!" someone else yelled.

"Hang him, now!" a few others joined in.

"You all just simmer down. There is gonna be no hangings until there is a proper trial."

"How many more folk are going to be poisoned before that time, Sheriff?" Doc Tuttle shouted. "Witchcraft! He could cast some terrible spells from his cell. Perhaps he should be burned like a witch!"

"Burn him! Burn him!" people chanted, as they began to swarm toward the front door.

Sheriff Ward had lost control and retreated into the office, locking the door behind him. Fists pounded on the door, while the frenzied townsfolk demanded instant justice. And instant justice for what, the Sheriff had to wonder. Somehow, and quite miraculously, people had been cured of their ailments after drinking Gabriel's elixirs. He needed answers and quickly.

"Your elixirs actually worked," the Sheriff stated, standing in front of Gabriel's cell.

"Just as I said they would."

"But…how? How is that possible?"

"Why should it matter, how? They work and that is the important thing."

"It matters because there is a mob of folk out there accusing you of witchcraft."

Gabriel shook his head in disbelief. "So, I have helped people. I have cured them of their maladies and now they are angry with me? They are healed, permanently."

"Folk become easily spooked by things they can't explain. You have done things that nobody else could achieve. They are scared and are looking for answers."

"Sheriff!" a voice was heard shouting from outside. "If you don't bring that stranger out here right now, we are gonna break this door down."

"What is it that they want?" Gabriel asked.

"They want to see you hang."

"But…I told you, I helped them. All I wanted to do was help them."

"And I told you, they are scared of things that cannot be explained. Would you care to explain to me how you can create elixirs that heal?"

Gabriel hung his head in defeat and sorrow. He let out a loud sigh before speaking again.

"I can see that this world is not yet ready for explanations, or help, for that matter."

"Huh? This world?"

"Humans are so mistrusting and so quick to anger. If you do not understand something, your first instinct is violence. I have done nothing more than to show kindness and heal those people in need, and now those same people wish to see me dead? As I said, this world is not ready. Perhaps myself, or others like me, will return here one day. Or, perhaps not. Maybe humans will never be ready. Farewell, Sheriff, I will leave you to your mob."

Sheriff Ward took a step back and shielded his eyes as a blinding, golden light, emanated from the stranger. Once the Sheriff was able to safely open his eyes again, he gasped. Gabriel still resembled Gabriel, but was outlined with a glowing, silvery radiance, and appeared almost translucent. Magnificent white wings sprouted from his back. The stranger nodded to the Sheriff before passing straight though the cell wall, like a ghost, and disappearing into the sky above.

Sheriff Ward stood frozen in place like a statue. He blinked his eyes several times and attempted to process what he had just witnessed. As the front door to his office threatened to burst open, from the repeated kicks of the angry mob, the man had to wonder how he would explain the missing prisoner.

SIR STEELHEART

I rode atop my muscled steed, along a lonely dark road. I was flanked on both sides by a murky swamp and the long weeping limbs of trees had blotted out most of the sunlight. I had grown somewhat accustomed to the stench by this point but the biting swamp flies threatened to push me over the edge of madness.

Fortunately, my horse, Ned, paid the flies no heed. Ned was as fine a horse as any; strong and fast and black as coal. I knew that Ned was his name and I knew that he was my horse, only I could not recall naming him or how he even came into my possession.

In fact, I was having trouble remembering anything of late. I was not sure why I was even on this road that cut through this accursed swamp. And where had I been before this? I could not recall. My memory was just a swirl of grey fog. Try and try as I might, I could remember nothing.

I shook my head in frustration and spurred Ned on to move a little more quickly. The sooner we exited this swamp the better. I knew of the ever-present dangers around me and kept my hand close to the hilt of my sword. Remaining in this swamp after the sun had disappeared was not a good idea at all. Trolls and things much worse than trolls prowled the swamps at night in these lands.

An hour or so later, Ned and I were granted a reprieve as the swamp gave way to an empty field of brownish grass. Mountains loomed like dark shadows in the distance and the lights from some kind of settlement could be seen near the base of the closest mountain. The sun had nearly disappeared, but I guessed that I could reach the settlement before it got too late, and kept Ned running at a steady pace.

It was clearly a town up ahead. It was protected by a high wall and I observed smoke rising from several chimneys within. With luck, I could find an inn to rest my weary bones and possibly get some answers as to my whereabouts.

I misjudged the distance of the town and darkness fell before reaching its gates. Two sentries armed with loaded crossbows looked down upon me from their stations along the wall.

"Who goes there?" one of them shouted.

"I am Sir Steelheart and I am in search of an inn."

"From where have you come?"

"I-I…don't know," I admitted.

"Drunk, already?"

"No. I am just having trouble with my memory, I apologize."

"Do you work for him?"

"I am sorry, work for who?"

"Darvaan, that sorcerous dog."

"No, I have never even heard that name before."

"Alright, we will open the gates but we are going to be keeping an eye on you. Do not attempt anything foolish."

"I wouldn't think of it. I need some cold ale and a place to rest my bones."

The front gates creaked open and another guard holding a spear motioned me in.

"You can leave your horse at the stables on your left, and that large building you see over there, that's the Flameguard Inn. You can get a drink and a meal and a small room there."

"My thanks."

I left Ned at the stables as instructed and made my way over to the inn. I could hear music from outside and was greeted to a busy taproom, bustling with activity, when I entered through the front door. A fair-sized crowd had assembled this night, and was being treated to entertainment provided by a bard, who was singing and playing the lute. Coins were scattered all over the floor around him, due to the intoxicated patrons who were unable to toss the coins into the man's hat that sat in front of him. Each time a new coin was tossed, the bard gave a slight nod without breaking a note from his song.

Several stools were vacant near the bar so I decided to choose one and sit myself down. I was dying to get out of my armor but quenching my thirst was my highest priority.

"A flagon of ale, please," I requested, once the

bearded man behind the bar had noticed me.

He was a large man with a grubby apron. He gave me a nod and fulfilled a few other orders before coming back my way and sliding over my drink.

"There you go, stranger. Five silver."

I took out six silver coins and deposited them onto the bar. I wore a pouch on my belt filled with gold and silver coins, though, for the life of me, I could not recall where I had earned them.

"Pardon me, my good man," I said to the barkeep, after downing my first mouthful of that much-needed drink. "What town is this?"

"Brockton. Not from around here, huh?"

"Ah, no, I am not."

"Well, welcome to Brockton, then. I am Bryan and I manage this establishment. What's your name, stranger?"

"Sir Steelheart."

"A Sir? You are one of the King's knights?"

"Ah, I am not sure."

"Eh? You have a title."

"This is true, but my memory is failing me of late."

In truth, I had no memory of where I had received that title, I just knew that it was indeed my name.

"Oh. I was hoping that you had been sent to save us."

"Save you from what?"

"That evil sorcerer that has been a plague upon these lands."

"Darvaan?"

"Ah, so you have heard of him?"

"Well, not really. One of the guards at the front gate had mentioned the name. What is the trouble?"

"That foul wizard has destroyed our crops and cursed our livestock in demand of gold. Each time he is paid, he grows greedier and demands even more the next time. The town cannot keep up with his demands, so he punishes us ever more."

"I see many capable-looking men in this room, as well as guards along the wall, why has nobody attempted to rid the world of this sorcerer?"

"Some have tried."

"And?"

"They were never seen again. The wizard is powerful."

I felt an anger boiling inside me. I did not know the folk in this town and yet I felt for them. Nobody should have to live under such tyranny. I was willing to bet these were all decent folk just struggling during the best of times.

"Where can this Darvaan be found?" I asked.

"He lives in a tower within the swamp, just south of here."

"Yes, I know that swamp all too well and was looking forward to never returning there."

"What are you saying? You will seek out this devil?"

"I cannot sit idly by while this is going on. Someone needs to put a stop to him. I feel as though that is why I am here."

"You are mad to go alone, Sir Steelheart. Nobody would fault you for leaving here and never coming back."

"I will seek out this tyrant and a put an end to your town's suffering, if I am able."

"Rest the night, at least. Your room and a warm meal will be on the house. It's the least I can do."

I accepted the barkeep's offer and after a delicious

meal, and another flagon of ale, I retired to a quiet room on the second floor of the inn. It was situated at the far end of the building. Far enough that I could no longer hear the songs of the bard or the voices of the other patrons. I lay in bed pondering my situation.

Again, I felt this overwhelming feeling that it was my duty to help these people whom I did not know. I felt that something had guided me to this town for this very reason. But what? And how? The barkeep mentioned a king, but I could not recall any king. I knew for certain that my name was indeed, Sir Steelheart, and that name did seem to belong to someone who would have been a knight in the employ of a king. I wish I knew what was going on. I wish I knew why I could not remember anything.

I tossed and turned and found little sleep that night. Strangely, though, I found that I was not worried about the prospect of facing some evil sorcerer who dwelled in that dreadful swamp. I felt confident that I could deal with this man when I found him. I was either extremely brave or extremely foolish, and I could not, at this point, say which.

That morning, I donned my armor, strapped on my sword, and exited the inn to a chorus of cheers from a gathered crowd. It appeared the barkeep had spread the word about my impending mission.

"May the gods bless you."

"Please save us."

"A thousand thank yous, Sir Steelheart."

"All hail, Sir Steelheart!"

The streets were thick with people, all witnessing my departure. I will admit it emboldened me even further. A young boy had already gotten a well-fed Ned ready for me, and had him waiting at the front gates. I mounted my faithful steed and gave one last wave to the townsfolk, before setting off through the gates.

As I traveled back the way I had come, back toward the swamp, I first considered the size of the swamp, and wondered where I would even begin my search. I had never noticed any tower from the main road and thought I could spend hours, or even days, in search of the sorcerer's home. But an odd feeling struck me. I felt as though I knew where to begin my search. It was as if that strange invisible force that had brought me to that town, was now guiding me in the right direction.

Long before reaching the swamp, I veered off the main road and took an alternate route. Within an hour's time, I reached that most unpleasant bog and noticed a pathway leading into its depths. It appeared seldom-trodden, but was definitely a path, all the same. I am not sure how I knew just where to locate this spot but perhaps the gods were guiding me on this noble quest.

The ground was uneven and fairly muddy, so I made the decision to leave Ned in the field and continue on foot. I did not bother to tether him to any tree, as I knew that Ned would wait for me to return.

Concern crept back into my mind, while I trudged through that horrendous landscape; concern over my failing memory. Why could I remember nothing from before the moment I found myself riding through this swamp the previous day? I have lived a life that eludes my recalling, no matter how hard I try. I know that I have lived for thirty-five years and yet I am not even sure as to how I know that. Where have I been for all that time? Why am I here now?

The harder I thought about it, the more frustrated it made me feel. I shook my head and decided to concentrate solely on the job before me. If Darvaan was indeed some terrible sorcerer, then I would need all my wits about me.

I hacked at rotten vines that almost appeared to reach for me, while doing my best not to inhale too much of the foul stench that permeated the air in this place. Swamps were not the loveliest of places to begin with but this particular one had to be among the worst. The smell of death and decay was almost unnatural and I was willing to wager it had something to do with this sorcerer. An awful necromancer would be my guess.

I worried at times, when I sunk nearly knee-deep into thick mud, but still I continued on, undaunted. After an hour into my torturous trek, the trees and reaching vines gave way to a small clearing. I was rewarded with the sight of a tall stone tower that rose straight out of the muck. The brick was as black as night. One single window was visible high up the tower.

I wondered if the sorcerer was aware of my approach, as their kind was apt to such knowledge. I frowned as the double doors to the tower suddenly flew open and a maniacal laugh confirmed my thought.

A black-robed man appeared in the doorway, where one did not exist a moment before. He held a long black staff in one skeletal hand. The hood of his robe concealed his face in darkness but two glowing red eyes were visible from within. A chill ran down my spine. I had found the sorcerer. He cackled and spoke with a raspy voice.

"So, Sir Steelheart, you come here thinking that…"

"How do you know my name?" I cut him off.

My question appeared to have given the sorcerer

pause. He stood in silence for a moment before speaking again.

"I will admit that I do not know how I know your name, but only that I do. You are Sir Steelheart, a meddlesome do-gooder who thinks he can just walk in here and save those pathetic townsfolk."

"You will leave those people alone from this day forward and you will leave these lands and never return. This deal I give you in exchange for your life."

Darvaan began that maniacal laugh once more and threw back the hood of his robe to reveal the head of a skull. "I abandoned my life long ago, foolish knight."

"I can destroy you all the same," I pronounced, as I drew my gleaming sword.

"You can try."

The sorcerer held his staff aloft and chanted in some unknown language. Before I could charge toward him, the muddied ground around me erupted, and several decayed corpses began to climb their way out.

"By all the gods," I whispered.

The blade of my sword was now glowing with a bluish hue and I did not hesitate in attacking the undead abominations. My weapon sliced through rotted flesh and bone as if it was mere butter. As I hacked three of the creatures to pieces, another three rose up from the ground. They scratched and clawed and bit at me, but could not penetrate my armor.

I sent ten of them back to their boggy graves before turning my attention, once again, to the sorcerer.

"Impressive indeed, Sir Foolheart," he taunted me. "But now you will die and become another of the undead guardians of my home."

He pointed a bony finger toward me and a bolt of
black energy flew forth. I held up my sword, confidently,
and stood my ground. The bolt of deadly magical energy
struck the blade of my sword and was immediately
absorbed into the weapon.

"My magical blade can absorb your spells, foul
wizard. Now, I will run you through."

I charged the evil thing before me and he shouted,
"NO!"

I raised my sword and brought it down with a
chopping motion. Darvaan held his staff out in a feeble
attempt to block my strike. My blade cut through his staff
with a shower of blue sparks and bit into a bony shoulder.
The sorcerer cursed and fell to the ground, just inside the
doorway to the tower.

I lifted my sword for a final strike and Darvaan
vanished. His laugh now echoed from everywhere around
me. It did not come from one place in particular but from
everywhere all at once.

"You have defeated me this time, Sir Foolheart, but
this is not over. One day, I will return and I will make you
pay for this."

His laughter faded into the distance and I knew the
sorcerer was gone. For now. I was certain that he would
indeed return and we would battle again. Somehow, I
knew that he and I were destined to be enemies forever,
and would have many more spectacular battles throughout
the coming years.

I made the journey back to the field where I had left
Ned and there he stood, patiently waiting for me, as I had
known he would. I returned to the town of Brockton and
was hailed as a hero during two days of celebration. I

allowed myself some enjoyment, but in the back of my mind, I knew I needed to remain vigilant. I knew that round two between Darvaan and I was not far off, and I needed to be ready.

*   *   *   *

"Michael? What are you doing in here, I have been calling you for five minutes? What is this you are working on? The Adventures of Sir Steelheart: Part One - The Sorcerer in the Swamp. Well, you certainly do have quite the imagination. I am happy to see that you are making good use of those pencil crayons we bought from that really strange woman at the garage sale. Anyhow, dinner is ready and is getting cold. Now, come down and eat and you can work on your comic book after."

THE FORTUNE TELLER

It was a wonderful summer's day without a cloud in the sky. I navigated my way through the crowded midway, while attempting to finish my ice cream before it melted and dripped all over my hand. I generally did not crave the frosty dessert but had observed some children indulging in the sinful sweets. I found that it was beyond my control to resist in purchasing my own. Mint chocolate chip was my favorite.

The carnival barkers were relentless as I passed the varied tents and game booths.

"Come on, sir, take your chance in the shooting gallery. Three shots for a nickel. Hit two or more ducks and win a prize."

"Right this way, mister. Ten cents to view the hideous lizard man. Half man, half lizard, all terrifying."

"This could be your lucky day. Just get the ball in the basket and you win a prize."

138

Perhaps a younger version of me might have been interested in playing games or taking a peek at the many oddities hidden away within the tents, but I was focused on finding only one attraction this day. I had already dallied enough by allowing the ice cream vendor to distract me. While I was enjoying the tasty treat, it was an unplanned detour from my course.

I am a writer for The Big City Times newspaper. I write the popular, Skeptical Skeptic column. As the title suggests, I am a profound skeptic and took immense delight in exposing various myths and fraudsters. "Stop the Bunk" was my famous catch phrase. Fortune Tellers were my preferred targets. They tended to irk me the most. Whether they claimed to be speaking with dead spirits returned or simply reading palms, I detested them all the same. Bottom dwellers, I considered them. Preying on the weak minded and foolish.

The Big City Summer Fair lasted the entire summer and lured out all types of charlatans. One in particular had gained my attention. Ms. Nayomi was a fortune teller who set up her own tent, a month past, at the opening of the fair. She had quite the reputation for accurate palm and card readings and I even had a few coworkers who swore she gave them accurate information. They claimed she must have possessed wonderful powers. My colleagues were not unintelligent folk and it continued to baffle me how even normal people were susceptible to the glib tongue of a trickster.

As I finished my ice cream, I spotted Ms. Nayomi's large red tent. Fortune Telling, Five Cents, the sign read. It amazed me that it was such a nominal fee to pay, for a look into your future. Who wouldn't be tempted? But of course, it's a large amount to pay when it's all false.

I had done some extensive investigative work prior to my arrival at the fair. Ms. Nayomi was really Natalie Schwartz, a former scientist with a large company based here in The Big City. The circumstances around her departure from the company were unclear but it appeared as though she may have quit. From scientist to fortune teller, that was an odd transition. Desperate times called for desperate measures, I suppose.

As I approached the tent, two giggling teens emerged from within. Looks of wonder were clearly evident upon their faces.

"I can't believe she knew all that," one girl said to the other.

"Ah, pardon me, girls, but you just had a reading with Ms. Nayomi?"

"Yes we did, both of us."

"And she was accurate, was she?"

"Oh my god, yes!" the brunette exclaimed. "She knew my name and even that tomorrow was my birthday!"

"Have you ever been here before? Seen Ms. Nayomi?"

"Never," the second girl answered. "We don't even live in The Big City. We took the train in from Floral Green, just to come to this fair for the first time."

"I see. Well, thank you both."

The girls walked away discussing their fortunes with excitement. The tent appeared empty of any other victims so I entered. The smell of burning incense immediately assaulted my nostrils. The smell wasn't unpleasant, but I did find it a little overwhelming. The inside of the tent was dimly-lit. There were no windows and only three candles set on the cluttered table in the middle of the reading area.

The table where Ms. Nayomi was seated was covered in a long red tablecloth, where sat decks of cards, a crystal ball, and other various knick-knacks and tools of the trade. The area where I stood was only half the size of the entire tent. The other half of the tent, behind where Ms. Nayomi sat, was curtained-off. A sign was hung stating that entry beyond the curtain was strictly prohibited.

Ms. Nayomi flashed me a welcoming smile. "Please, sir, have a seat."

She looked very much like I imagined she would. She wore a long black gown with large gaudy earrings hanging from both ears. Several chains also hung around her neck and each of her fingers was ornamented with jeweled rings. Fake jewels, of course. Her lipstick was black and matched her black hair, which she wore back in a ponytail. She appeared somewhere in her forties and was mildly attractive. Of course, the whole fortune telling thing lessened a person's look in my eyes, but I suppose if I had spotted her dressed normally, at a dinner party, or perhaps the picture show, she might have caught my fancy.

I did as instructed and took a seat opposite her at the table. I grinned like a foolish child who was here to eat up whatever slop she was about to dish out. I placed my nickel on the table beside her silly crystal ball.

"So, Bradley, are you interested in your future, or are you looking for guidance with your love life? What can I interest you in today?"

I stopped short from blurting out my first reply, as to why a fortune teller was asking me what I was interested in, since she should have already known, but something else caught me off guard.

"You know my name, so obviously you have recognized me."

"I am sorry, no, I have never seen you before."

"Sure you haven't. You must read The Big City Times and recognized my face from my column."

"As strange as it might sound, no, I do not actually read the Times. I get all the information I need, elsewhere."

"Right. So of all the names in the world, you correctly guessed mine? Amazing."

"Well, you have the feel of a Bradley."

That made me laugh. I felt like a Bradley.

"Alright, continue. Tell me my future."

"I sense you came here for other reasons, really, and not to hear about your future. You are somewhat skeptical, aren't you?"

"Somewhat?" I chuckled. "That's putting it mildly. You are clearly familiar with the column I write."

"I have never read it before, I told you. Believe it or not, I have never even read the magazine you wrote for before you joined the Times."

"Ah, I see now. One of my coworkers has given you some background on me in a vain attempt to impress me," I stood up then. "This is pointless. Someone is playing a joke on me. I will find out who."

"Don't you want to get even a small glimpse into your future before leaving?" she asked, as I had turned to exit.

"Not really, but go ahead anyway."

She closed her eyes in some ridiculous gesture of meditating and then opened them a moment later. "Bring a spare shirt to work tomorrow."

"What is that supposed to mean?"

"Enjoy the rest of your day, Bradley. Maybe even get a second mint chocolate chip ice cream since that is your favorite flavor."

I stormed out of the tent and headed straight home. I was fuming. Some office prankster was trying to sabotage my piece on Ms. Nayomi. My first instinct told me it was Frieda. She seemed offended when I laughed at her for believing in the fortune teller. I must have offended her so she went back and gave the clever woman information about me to try and convince me of her powers. That was it.

Of course as Monday morning arrived, Frieda denied all accusations and even feigned being more offended than she had been previously. In fact, the entire office denied any accountability over the information Ms. Nayomi had acquired.

I sat at my desk stewing. Perhaps it wasn't anyone here. It was obvious she knew my name from the paper and had recognized me from a photo. It was not secret information that I had worked for a magazine before coming to the Times. Anyone could dig that up with a little effort. And as for the ice cream, well, she must have seen me eating it before I entered her tent. It would be a simple assumption that I would have purchased my favorite flavor. Either she had seen me eating it, or more likely, she had an accomplice that watched people outside the tent. Someone that probably stayed hidden behind that curtained-off area.

The phone on my desk rang and pulled me from my contemplations. As I grabbed the receiver, I accidentally knocked over my cup of coffee and spilled the entire contents onto the front of my white shirt. Fortunately, the coffee had long since gone cold, but my shirt was soaked and stained. I cursed to myself and then suddenly remembered Ms. Nayomi's words.

"Bring a spare shirt to work tomorrow."

But how? I could see if someone was in on the joke and they had spilled the coffee on my shirt but I had done this myself. Or did someone strategically place my coffee mug closer to the edge of the desk, during a brief moment of absence. That was it.

"Ha ha, very funny everyone," I announced.

"Wow, look at your shirt," Francis said. "You are very clumsy."

"Yes, look at my shirt. Was it you, Francis? Was it?"

"Was it me, what?"

"She put you up to this, didn't she? You moved the mug on my desk, huh?"

"I beg your pardon? I have been at my desk all morning."

I heard Neil laughing. "It was you, then, Neil? You think this is funny?"

"I didn't do anything but yeah I think it is pretty funny. This woman has really gotten into your head. I guess she does have a gift."

"No!" I shouted. "She does not have a gift. One of you did this, I know it."

The following day I left the office in the morning and spent three hours watching Ms. Nayomi's tent from a distance. I remained out of sight, standing between the tent of the bearded lady and a stall selling caramel apples. I watched for anyone suspicious coming or going from the tent, someone that could have been in league with Ms.

Nayomi. I saw nobody. Ms. Nayomi never emerged from the tent at any time either.

Frustrated, I waited for the latest victim to leave the tent before entering again.

"So, who is in on this? Francis? Neil? Herbert? Which one?"

"In on what, exactly?" she feigned ignorance.

"Don't play dumb with me."

"Are you going to stand there accusing me of nonsense, or are you going to sit down for a reading? We both already know you are going to sit down."

I took a seat. "Fine. Tell me something else that is going to happen."

"That will cost you five cents, Mr. Fluke."

"Oh right, you have never read my column before. I guess I also feel like a Fluke, huh?" I tossed a nickel on the table. "There. Amaze me."

I snorted as she cupped her crystal ball with both hands and gazed into nothingness.

"Can you get tonight's boxing match on that thing? My radio at home has been acting up."

She ignored my comment and continued with her absurd spectacle.

"I see you are on the east side of the city tomorrow. A meeting, perhaps?" My eyes narrowed. "Wait, I see you standing beside your car. You are not happy. One of your tires is flat."

I had a meeting on the east side of the city tomorrow, concerning an article I was planning to write but I had not told anyone in the office about that yet. How could she have known? Who would have told her?

"What color is my car?"

"Blue."

I marched out of the tent without another word. Someone was playing games with me and I was not impressed with this. Someone must have been spying on me or going through my appointment book, which was locked in my desk drawer at the office.

The next morning, before leaving for my meeting, a thought struck me and I inspected every inch of every tire on my car. I was certain someone would have stuck a nail in one, or possibly slashed it; done something to cause a flat. I could detect nothing with the naked eye but that didn't mean there wasn't a small hole somewhere, causing a slow leak. So, I stopped at the closest gas bar and filled each tire with air, to be on the safe side.

I was about ten minutes from my appointed destination, when an oblivious kid, stupidly rode his bicycle off the sidewalk and into my path. I swerved just in time to avoid the boy and ran into the curb with a loud thump. I honked and cursed, simultaneously, then jumped out to inspect the damage. My front passenger tire was ruined. Flat.

The boy rode his bike over to where I stood.

"Gee, mister, I am sorry. I swear I didn't see you coming."

I grabbed him roughly by the arm. "Did she tell you to do that? She told you to ride in front of me, knowing I would have to swerve?"

"W-what? She, who?"

"Tell me!" I shouted.

"Mister, you are hurting my arm."

I let the boy go and told him to beat it. He couldn't ride away fast enough. Needless to say, I missed my meeting. It was nearly an hour before I got the spare tire on my car, and by that time, the individual I was to meet had given up and departed.

The next day, I was once again seated across from Ms. Nayomi. I slapped a nickel on the table, as she was reluctant to answer any questions until I had done so.

"I could have killed that boy. You told him to ride in front of me?"

"I have done no such thing, Mr. Fluke. I saw the flat tire in your future, nothing more."

"You couldn't have known that would happen unless you planned it!"

"Please, lower your voice. I am a fortune teller, this is what I do."

"You were a scientist, not a fortune teller. What did you do for IvoryTech before leaving, Ms. Schwartz? Yes, I know all about you too. I must be a fortune teller myself, eh? You graduated with honors from right here at the Big City University. A brilliant mind, by all accounts. A budding scientist. Now you sit here in a tent, next to the cotton candy stand, and you peddle in deceit at a fair."

"I realized that wasn't the life for me. I had a gift, so I decided to pursue that."

"Your only gift was your understanding of technology and your intelligence. You cannot read minds or see into my future. It is all a scam, Ms. Schwartz. I have been debunking this rubbish for years."

"Because you don't believe in it, it immediately becomes rubbish, does it?"

"It's rubbish because that is indeed what it is. Rubbish."

"Very well, you are entitled your opinion."

"Look into your little magic ball there and tell me something else," I tossed a second nickel onto the table.

The woman sighed and again proceeded with her laughable performance with the ball. When her eyes opened, she spoke.

"I am afraid I see your father, he is in distress."

"Oh, he is, is he? He is quite healthy for his age, with no signs of leaving this existence any time soon."

"I just see him in a hospital bed, that is all."

That weekend, when my mother called to say that my father had been feeling very ill and was taken to the hospital, I rushed right over. The doctors suspected food poisoning. From the hospital, I drove straight to the fair.

"You poisoned my father in order to convince me?" I accused.

"Excuse me?"

"My father is in the hospital, as you said, sick with possible food poisoning."

"Yes, I saw that scene. I told you."

"I know you told me. So you had him poisoned, didn't you? I will have you arrested and locked away for this."

"Calm down, Mr. Fluke. I haven't gone anywhere near your father."

"You had someone do it?"

"I work alone."

"Sure you do," I threw a nickel on the table. "Tell me what you are planning next. What do you see this time?"

"There is no need to behave in this manner."

"Tell me."

She proceeded with her carnival act once more and I laughed at the incredulity of it all. This time she wore a

148

mask of confusion, as if something troubled her. She shook her head and looked again. The same expression remained.

"Your magic ball is not working? Want me to fix the antenna on the roof? Might be a reception issue."

"I don't see any future. It's all just white. I don't understand."

"What does that mean? It's all just white?"

"It means simply that. Inside the ball is white, everywhere I look, it's just white. That is all I can see, nothing more."

"I should demand my nickel back but I think you are in more need of it than I am."

Disgusted, I turned to leave as a woman was entering at the same time.

"I am sorry, miss," Ms. Schwartz said. "Do you mind coming back in about fifteen minutes?"

"She has to fix her magic ball," I commented on my way out.

I was about halfway to my car, when I turned back around. I found another place to sit out of sight and watched the tent. This time I was going to wait until Ms. Schwartz left. I was curious to see where she would go or who she would speak with. Hours passed and she never left once. Pitiful victims came and went, each emerging with expressions of awe.

Night was falling and the fair was beginning to close. I had waited hours and Ms. Schwartz did not appear. The tent went dark and she still had not made an exit.

With my patience worn out completely, I marched into the tent. It took a moment for my eyes to adjust to the darkness but there was some light coming from behind the curtain that cut the tent in half. Perhaps, Ms. Schwartz slept overnight on the other side. It was time for a peek. What was she hiding over there?

I approached the curtain, when a sudden flash of light, and a loud crackling sound, actually sent me to the floor on my buttocks, out of fright. The flash momentarily blinded me and once my vision returned, I stood and pulled the curtain aside. I was stunned by the scene in front of me.

There was no other exit from the tent and yet there was no Ms. Schwartz. It was as if she had simply vanished. A small table was the only furnishing on this side of the tent. On that table sat the weirdest contraption I had ever laid eyes upon. It had buttons and dials and two objects that appeared to be handles. As I moved in for a closer inspection, I could see a small screen right above a series of numbered buttons. Displayed on the screen was a date. I had to think for a moment but the date was tomorrow's date. Just what in the hell was this thing?

*   *   *   *

"Hey, Frieda, have you seen Bradley today? I have looked all over the office."

"You mean you didn't hear?"

"Hear what? I was in a meeting all morning. He is home sick?"

"He was picked up by the police last night."

"The police? For what?"

"Well, as I heard it, at first they thought him wandering around drunk. He was babbling incoherently."

"I didn't think Bradley even drank."

"He doesn't. Apparently they found nothing in his

system but he continued to babble and make not a word of sense all night long. I heard he was admitted to the Big City Asylum and is sitting in one of those white padded rooms."

"Goodness, me. He hasn't said anything at all that has made sense? Nothing to explain what happened?"

"Nothing, as I heard it. They found him not far from the fair, and he keeps going on and on, babbling about time travel."

THE GRAVE OF OLD MAN FINKEL

Journal Entry #167 – June 4

I had no luck again today. I spent thirteen hours standing in that barren river, panning for gold, that would appear does not exist. I suppose it is the varied tales of men striking it rich in these parts that keeps me going, but I have yet to find even the smallest amount of gold. Do I regret leaving my farm? Every day. The work was hard and the hours long but it put food in my mouth. What little money I have brought with me is nearly spent. All the tools I have bought have so far proven useless. I had even purchased a large wagon, dreaming that I would require it to carry all my gold back into town. A fool's dream, perhaps. I have traveled too far to give up just yet. Tomorrow is another day. I will venture further up river in the morning and see if my luck changes.

Journal Entry #168 – June 6

I stood in that gods-forsaken river until well after dark tonight with nothing to show for it but a grumbling stomach. I encountered two other prospectors that had also met with the same luck as I. I can't be doing this wrong as there is no other way to be doing it. Using that stupid pan to sift through the mud at the bottom of the river. I traveled further north the last two days, for all the good that did me. It was at Johnson's Bend where I crossed paths with Alfred and Benjamin. At first the meeting was tense and my hand drifted to the handle of my six-shooter. Gold prospectors were generally territorial, but seeing as how they had also found nothing, I was not viewed as any sort of threat. We exchanged depressing tales and agreed to share a fire and some drinks tonight. I am off to join them at their campsite.

Journal Entry #169 – June 7

Another fruitless day, I regret to report. Thank god for the willow tree that offered me some relief from that awful midday sun. At least I am not alone with my misfortune. I learned last night that Alfred and Benjamin are also in dire straits. Both left decent-paying jobs and gambled everything on traveling to this region to make a fortune in gold. Like me, their dreams have been dashed with weeks of nothing to show for their work. Alfred even left a wife and children behind, with the thought of returning to them a rich man. My food stores are running drastically low. I can't afford to waste time making the two-day trek back into town. Additionally, I have almost no money left to replenish my supplies. I don't know how much longer I can last out here.

Journal Entry #170 – June 11

I have not written for several days now. Recent events have unnerved me and I have gotten very little rest. I have been sleeping with one eye open and with my six-shooter resting on my chest. Two days ago, I came across a grisly discovery. I found Benjamin hanging from the branch of a willow tree, overlooking the river. A handwritten note was left nearby, stating that he had gambled everything and lost. He no longer possessed the will to continue and felt shamed to return home empty-handed. Poor Benjamin. I attempted to locate Alfred but his partner was nowhere to be found. I waited near their camp until nightfall but the other man never returned. I felt conflicted, but with the death of Benjamin and the disappearance of Alfred, I helped myself to what little food and drink they had left at their campsite. The following day, while continuing my futile search for gold, Alfred appeared from behind a tree and nearly put a bullet in my head. The man looked disheveled, and fortunately, his shaky hand spoiled his aim, causing that bullet to whiz past my ear without harm. I ran for the woods as he fired two more times, while shouting that I was a dirty thief. We have been playing a game of hide and seek ever since. I know he is still out here, searching for me. I can hear him still, from time to time. I do not wish to kill the man who is clearly distraught by the death of his friend, but I will be damned if I am going to let him shoot me. The food I took from their camp is nearly gone. I think I am going to be forced to journey back into town. Maybe tomorrow I will attempt to catch some fish.

Journal Entry #171 – June 12

Well, that lunatic Alfred forced me to kill him today. While I was trying to catch some fish, which proved a waste a time, Alfred found me. Thankfully, I was fast on the draw and was able to shoot him dead. I didn't want to kill him. I was hoping we could have talked but he was beyond reason. I found some money in his pockets but there was regrettably no food in his possession. I spent two hours burying the man. I think I will leave for town in the morning. I cannot go much longer without any food. Clearly, I am no fisherman. What a nightmare my life has become. I considered bringing the bodies of both men into town but I do not wish to have any suspicion placed on me. Benjamin obviously killed himself and I killed Alfred in self-defence, but that could be difficult to prove with no witnesses. It is best that I leave them out here and claim no knowledge of their whereabouts, if ever brought to question.

Journal Entry #172 – June 13

It would appear that I have been the victim of thieves. All the money I owned, down to the last coin, was missing as I awoke this morning. Footprints led away from my camp and disappeared in the woods. I know this region is thick with would-be prospectors and thievery is not uncommon. I will have to postpone my trip to town. With no money to purchase food, it would be a useless journey. I will have to find food somehow and keep up the search for gold. That is the only chance I have.

Journal Entry #173 – June 15

No gold. I am convinced now that this river hides no fortune below its watery surface. I am starving and cannot last much longer. I may have to consider selling what little equipment I have in town, in order to buy food. My wagon is worth a few meals at least. A small part of me still clings to the irrational thought that if I stay just a little longer, I am bound to find gold. That is the gold fever talking. It is a sickness, I realize now, but a sickness that is hard to shake. I am feeling weaker. No more can I write this evening. I need rest.

Journal Entry #174 – June 16

I have done something despicable today. I hate myself for it but it has bought me a few more days to remain at the river in search of gold. I packed up my gear this morning and headed onto the road leading back to town. An hour into my journey, I came across a stagecoach. There was three well-to-do travelers plus the driver. Without even thinking it through, I drew my gun and robbed them. They stopped to offer me a ride into town but I robbed them of a few days' worth of food and some cash. I have since returned to my campsite and spent the rest of the afternoon panning for gold. I found nothing today but I have to find something soon. I just have to.

Journal Entry #175 – June 19

I find myself once again questioning my sanity. The food I robbed from the stage is gone and I have found no gold in this rotten river. This river will be the death of me, I am certain of it. I am beginning to believe that either all the gold that was here is gone, or I was provided false information and there was none in this region to begin with. I have found several abandoned campsites, which lead me to believe that others have already been here ahead of me and taken whatever there was here to find. Or, they had more sense than me and knew when to give up and leave. Each time I decide I have had enough, a nagging feeling tells me to wait just a little longer. I am trying to show patience but my patience is wearing dreadfully thin.

Journal Entry #176 – June 20

This morning I found a most curious item floating down the river. It was a clear bottle and I almost paid it no mind. As it floated past, I noticed there was a piece of paper inside. Naturally, I scooped it up and pulled out the paper to find out what it was. It was a letter. The handwriting was almost illegible but I believe I was able to decipher it. It was written by a prospector, like myself. The man claims that he struck it rich, finding a major deposit of gold up river. He goes on to say that he received major injuries in a bear attack. He forced the bear to flee but he believes he will succumb to his injuries. A poorly drawn map was included at the bottom of the letter. The man says that he has hidden his gold in an old graveyard near the river. He placed it in the grave of Old Man Finkel. He ends the letter by saying that he will attempt to crawl to the road for help but does not truly believe that he will make it. He hopes that somebody will find this letter and the gold will not go to waste. Dirty fingerprints were found all over the paper and also contributed to a difficult read. The letter is not dated, so I have no idea how long ago this was written. But the fact that I found the letter still within the bottle, makes me believe that I am the first to read this. According to the map, this graveyard is about a half-day travel from my current location. I will attempt to get a good sleep this night and set out at first light.

Journal Entry #177 – June 21

It is late in the afternoon and I have located the graveyard. There is approximately sixty headstones spread out in an area fairly close to the river. Using the poorly drawn map, I was able to locate the grave of Old Man Finkel easily enough. The grave is open and a plain wooden coffin rests inside the hole. I observed many footprints throughout the graveyard but nothing to indicate that anyone had recently visited the grave of Old Man Finkel. I firmly believe the gold must still be intact within the casket. I passed several other prospectors down river, not far from here. I do not wish anyone to see me opening a coffin in the graveyard. I have decided to return to the grave later tonight and conduct my business in the dark, away from prying eyes.

Journal Entry #178 – June 22

It is well past midnight and I firmly believe that there is

nobody else in the vicinity. I have heard nothing save for the sound of the river and the chirping of crickets. There is no glow from any campfires. I believe my luck has finally changed. I am starving and this is my last-ditch effort to salvage anything from this expedition. The author of the letter mentioned he had found a fortune in gold. Now, all I have to do is retrieve it from that grave. I am leaving now. I will write again when I return with good news.

*   *   *   *

The undead creature finished eating the last remaining bit of the unfortunate prospector and tossed his clothing behind a thick bush. Filthy and rotted fingers placed the letter back into the bottle and it shambled over to the river, tossing the bottle in. Through black pits for eyes, it watched as the bottle floated down the river and out of sight. Satisfied, the horrible thing returned to the grave of Old Man Finkel. It climbed back inside the coffin to await the arrival of its next meal.

HAROLD THE CONQUEROR

I sheathed my sword and entered the keep when I was told the fighting was over. Greymane Keep was the seat of power for Baron Stromwall but Baron Stromwall was no more. Three hours after storming the immense keep, the Baron and his forces had been defeated. My brothers and I had won.

Our victory was never in doubt. Stromwall was weak and foolishly thought to rule these lands with kindness and compassion. Two qualities that should never be attributed to a ruler. People were more inclined to work harder and talk less when motivated by fear. I wonder if Stromwall came to realize his folly just before my brother Curtis removed his head.

A soldier approached me and it was obvious that he was fresh from battle. Blood still dripped from his silver armor but he himself showed no wounds. He bowed his head and took a knee in front of me.

"My Lord, the entire keep is secure and Lords Curtis and Stephan await you in the throne room."

I nodded and waved the man away. I took my time, strolling through the hallways, admiring the carnage around me. My brothers could wait. A lord never hurried.

"Oh, look who has finally arrived now that the battle is won," my brother Curtis said, once the three of us were alone in the throne room.

"Not a drop of blood on his armor," Stephan added, with a sneer.

Their verbal barbs did no harm. "Someone had to ensure that nobody escaped this keep. My men and I had the place surrounded. Can you imagine the chaos that would ensue if Stromwall had somehow gotten away?"

Curtis laughed. "A convenient excuse, dear brother. There was no hope of escape for that weakling."

"Underground tunnels, perhaps? We don't know the full layout of this place."

Stephan rolled his eyes. "You are always late to battle. It is always one thing or another. You never want to dirty your hands. I have half a mind to call you a cow…"

I placed a hand on the pommel of my sword and cut him off right there. "Careful, brother. Choose your words wisely."

"Or what? You plan on running me through?"

Curtis stepped between us. "Enough with the bickering. We have won and that is all that matters. Now we have to focus on the King and his reaction to our coup."

"As long as we can convince the King that we have no ambitions beyond Stromwall's lands, there should be no need to fear any retaliation," I figured. "Our forces are too large for the King to easily defeat us, so the intelligent route is to accept us as the new barons and life continues on much as it did before. The higher taxes we will impose, will only mean more coins in his coffers."

"He has a point, I hate to say," Stephan reluctantly agreed. "Stromwall was too lax in his rule and the King was ultimately losing wealth as a result. That greedy pig of a man shouldn't care who rules this region as long as he sees more coins flowing over to him."

Curtis nodded. "Alright, maybe we send a nice tribute over immediately, as a friendly gesture? It won't take long for him to hear of what happened to Stromwall, so it's in our best interest to make first contact and start things off on good terms."

"Once we locate the vault in this place, I will assemble some trusted men to make the delivery."

"Excellent, Stephan," Curtis smiled. "Tonight we feast and celebrate like barons."

I was not one for celebrations and ducked out early that evening, just as the alcohol consumption was reaching an epic level. I decided to lay claim to one of the better bedrooms in the keep before Stephan could. Stromwall's room now belonged to Curtis. Curtis was the biggest and strongest of us three, and by far, the fiercest warrior. We all agreed to rule as equals, but some things still went to the strongest. That was just the way of the world and the chief reason Stromwall was now without his head. He was weak, so the strong swept him aside. There was no place here for people like him. The strong is entitled to take what they want and that is exactly what we did. After two years of planning, the keep and these lands were ours.

As I explained to my brothers, the King should not

become a worry of ours. Stromwall was a fool. In an act of insane kindness, he lowered the taxes of the people living in this region. He lowered the taxes on merchants operating in this region. He wanted to make life easier on the people and alleviate their suffering. He gave away lands owned by the crown. He reduced punishments for many of the petty crimes that ran rampant in this region. What manner of man would do such a thing? A man unfit to rule, that was who.

My brothers were more brawn than brain. They could take the keep and hold onto it but I would suggest the best ways to govern. There is going to be a considerable tax increase on everyone, for starters. Merchants are going to be taxed heavily and will also need to purchase a permit to sell anything within this region. And the death penalty will be imposed on all crimes, no matter how petty. The folk in these parts are going to learn very quickly that we are not to be trifled with.

I found the second largest bedroom on the top level of the keep to my liking. The previous owner would have no more use for it. We had Stromwall's brother executed before the celebrations began. The skinny fop had surrendered during the battle but I suggested that no person from this keep be left alive. The room was large enough for my needs but the décor would need to change. The bed, however, was indeed quite comfortable.

I lounged around for some time before sleep eventually overtook me. I spent that time considering the future. We had taken over Stromwall's keep with such ease, that it made me think that we could turn our attention to other barons. Targeting the King at this point was far too great an ambition to undergo, but it was not entirely out of the question in the future. I thought if we removed several other barons first, then we could amass the men and the wealth necessary to dethrone the King.

Men flocked to my brothers and me. We may have been born into a poor family but we were also born to rule. It was just a part of our very souls. Soldiers listened to us and rallied to our cause. To this point, we had gathered men with great promises. Now that we had captured the keep, we had the coins to make good on those promises, and this was just the beginning.

My brothers would be satisfied with just ruling Stromwall's region but I had much grander goals in mind. Curtis would be the easier of my two brothers to convince. The man loved fighting more than anything else in life. He was a brute that stood several inches taller than I and built like a stone house. If he believed that victory would be ours, then his bloodlust would secure his compliance. Stephan, on the other hand, would be more difficult.

Stephan and I butted heads often. Most of the time he argued with me just for the sake of arguing. If I made a suggestion, he would take the opposite stance, just for the sole reason that it was my idea. He was a year older than me, and had the mind that since he was the oldest, he should ultimately be in charge. He hated that I was the smarter of the two of us. I was positive that Stephan would be happy with what we had gained so far and not wish to press our luck further. He would be a problem.

The next few weeks went well during the transition of power. The people in these lands came to know that we now ruled and we meant business. I ordered the dungeons emptied and we held a mass hanging in front of the keep, to rid ourselves of prisoners. Why should we waste perfectly good food to feed criminals? Word spread that we would no longer arrest criminals; they would be executed on the spot. That order had been carried out a half-dozen times already to prove that this was no jest.

After a month of tense waiting, a messenger arrived with the news we had been hoping for. The King did express his disapproval of our methods of deposing Baron Stromwall, but there would be no action taken against us. The King accepted our tribute and would be expecting more where that came from. He would get his coins, for the time being.

As expected, Stephan made agreeing on any plans extremely difficult. He fought me every step of the way, simply because I had thought of them. And it came as no surprise to me that he was opposed to eliminating the barons closest to us.

One cool night, I found my troublesome brother pacing the battlements of the keep.

"Do you hear that, brother?" I asked.

"Hear what? I don't hear anything."

"Precisely. There is nothing but silence out there."

"And your point?"

"The people in these lands have fallen in line. They are too busy working hard for us all day long, to drink and revel at night. They are sleeping, so that they may wake early and begin their work day anew."

"And if we expand, as you suggest, it will be harder to keep everyone in line. Be happy with what we have."

"Why should we settle with what we now have, when we could have more?"

"Because Stromwall was a fool and never saw us coming. The other barons are already fearful of our potential ambitions and are no doubt preparing for us, in the event of us wishing to expand. Do not think that everyone will be so easily defeated."

"Bah! We have the men and the coins to buy more men. None of these barons could resist us."

"And what of the King? You think that he will just sit idly by and watch us slowly take over all his lands?"

"Soon enough, the King won't be able to stop us either."

"No. I will never agree to your plans. This region is large enough for us to rule and live as kings, anyhow. That is good enough for me."

"We could have more," I implored. "So much more."

"Not interested in your ideas of conquest."

"Fine. But you see that solider down there in the courtyard?"

Stephan leaned over, squinting his eyes. "Which one?"

"That one. The one right below you."

As my brother leaned over a little further, I grabbed him by his shirt and threw him off the battlement. His scream was cut short as his body broke against the ground of the courtyard. I spotted the closest solider to me, patrolling the battlements, and an idea quickly came to mind.

"Guards! Guards!" I shouted. "There has been an assassination! Guards!"

The closest guard arrived first, wearing a mask of confusion. I drew my sword and cut a line of blood across his left arm. He jumped back with a yelp. Three more guards rushed to our position and I pointed my blade at the wounded soldier.

"This man has killed my brother! Take him!"

"My Lord?" the bleeding man went pale. "I did no such thing. I ran over here as soon as you shouted."

I ignored him and continued to address the others. "He pushed Lord Stephan over the side! Drag him to the dungeon. He is a Stromwall sympathizer!"

The soldier was disarmed and roughly taken away. He shouted his innocence the entire way. Approximately an hour later, Curtis found me in the corridor outside my bedroom. Blood was splattered on the white shirt he wore.

"Would you like to know what that soldier said while we tortured him?" he asked me.

"What?"

"Nothing."

"Nothing?"

"He maintained his innocence, right until the moment he died."

"Who knew that Stromwall had such fanatical supporters?"

"Yes, brother, who knew?"

"We will need to be more mindful of traitors in our midst."

"Indeed. I suppose it had nothing to do with the fact that Stephan opposed your ideas of expansion?"

"How dare you accuse me of murdering our brother. Despite our differences, he was still family."

"I sincerely hope you would do no such thing, since I oppose your plan as well."

"What? Baron Eriksson is the perfect target for our next move. He will crumble before us and his region will be ours."

"And then the King will sweep through here and

crush us. Stephan was right. We have all the land and wealth we need right here. Enjoy it, brother. We only have to divide things two ways now."

Curtis took his leave and I stood there for some time, immensely disappointed by his words. I was certain that he would see things my way and be eager to get out there and fight. This was going to be a serious problem. I took a brief moment to consider that nameless soldier. Did I feel bad that an innocent man was tortured to death for my crime? No. It was necessary. He was just a small pawn in the grand scheme of things. I slept just fine that night.

Curtis proved to be the new thorn in my side over the course of the following few weeks. His attitude toward me had changed. He constantly threw out comments that implicated me in Stephan's murder. He was certain that I was behind it.

I never shed a tear when I was informed that Curtis was murdered. Another of Stromwall's supporters had poisoned him, or so the story went. He was adamant in his opposing stance of attacking the other barons so he had to go. I would have preferred to have both my brothers beside me in the coming wars but it was not meant to be. They did not share my visions of conquest. It was truly unfortunate.

A year later, I was touring the new lands under my control, following the defeat of Baron Eriksson. I dismounted my horse and approached a haggard-looking woman who refused to bow before me and just glared with pure hatred.

"This is your farm?" I asked her.

"Yes it is," she spat. "All mine since my husband died. Worked to death."

"You will take a knee when faced with your Lord."

"I see no Lord here. Just an evil tyrant."

My patience was wearing thin. "You should rejoice. Your previous baron was weak. Now, you have a strong leader who is capable of protecting your land."

"It won't be my land for much longer. I can't keep up with your taxes."

"A pity."

I snapped my fingers and two soldiers shoved the woman into the mud, forcing her to kneel before me.

"Next time, I will not be as forgiving," I warned her.

I turned back toward my horse and that witch produced a blade from under her dress and dove at me. My guards were too slow to react and she drove that blade hilt-deep into my back. I shrieked in agony and fell to my knees. My men threw her back down in the mud and began to beat her near senseless. With unimaginable pain, I pulled the dagger from my back and rose to my feet, seething with anger. I approached her, grimacing with every painful step.

"Any last words before I cut your throat?"

"Yes! A curse upon you, you horrible tyrant! I curse you to suffer in this life and every life you live after this one!"

*   *   *   *

"Alright, Harold, I am going to count to three and snap my fingers, and then you will open your eyes. One. Two. Three."

SNAP.

"Hey, Doc. Did it work? Did you find out anything

useful? This pain in my back is something terrible."

"Ummm…"

"No? Geez, no medical doctors can ever explain my pain. I was really hoping your hypnosis thing could help me remember if I ever injured it somehow and just plum forgot."

"Well, Harold, I really specialize in past life regression. Under hypnosis, I generally bring people a lot farther back in time than what you were hoping. Do you have any brothers, by chance?"

"Yes, two. My older brother has a gift for arguing and actually became a lawyer. My younger brother is a brute of a man and is a professional boxer. We never really got along and I don't talk to them much. Why?"

"Oh, just wondering is all. Sometimes chronic pain can run in the family. I was just curious if your brothers suffered from the same pain."

"No, not that I am aware of. This pain is really affecting my work, Doc. Makes it so difficult to bend over when I clean the toilets at the schools."

"Maybe you need a longer handle on your brush?"

DINNER AT THE
WAINWRIGHT'S

Robert Wainwright paced back and forth in his living
room, occasionally glancing outside the front window. It
was a quiet Sunday and the afternoon was quickly turning
into evening. He was about to take a seat and pick up a
magazine, when a sound drew his attention back to the
window. He spotted a vehicle pulling into his driveway and
he called out.

"Dear, the King's have arrived."

Prescilla Wainwright emerged from the kitchen and
inspected her dress and hair in front of a mirror. Once
satisfied, she joined her husband at the front door just as
the doorbell chimed.

"Well, go on, open the door," Prescilla urged, after
her husband had hesitated.

Robert inhaled deeply, nodded to his wife, and then
opened the door, while wearing his biggest smile.

"Good evening, George, Clara, you found the place, alright?"

"Of course, ole sport," George King replied.

Clara rolled her eyes. "Now, George…"

"Alright, well, we may have made a few wrong turns but a chap at the gas bar down the road pointed us in the right direction. We just don't get out into the country very often. You know, life in the Big City."

"Understandable, yes. Well, do come in, won't you?"

The King's were invited in and prompted to take a seat in the living room.

"Dinner will be ready shortly," Priscilla announced, before disappearing back into the kitchen.

"It's good to see you both again. What has it been? Two years? Three?"

George had to think for a moment. "Closer to three, I would have to say."

"The last time we saw you and Prescilla was at that art show," Clara added. "So, yes, three years."

"Time just flies, doesn't it?"

"You've got that right, Rob," George agreed. "How are you adjusting to life in the country?"

"Quite well, actually. It's quiet out here. As you have noticed there is no traffic out this way. The pace is very slow and leisurely. We like it."

"The scenery on the way here was lovely, I must say," Clara commented.

"Indeed, so. After we eat we can give you a tour around. The lake in the back offers a breath-taking view. There is nothing like sitting by the lake with a coffee in the morning."

"Dinner is ready," Prescilla called. "Bring our guests

to the dining room, Rob."

Robert guided his guests into the dining room where Prescilla had set a marvelous table. Fresh buns right out of the oven. Salad with a savory dressing. Shrimp galore. And a mouth-watering main dish of roasted chicken with mashed potatoes and mixed vegetables as a side.

"This looks fantastic, Prescilla."

"Thank you, Clara. Sit wherever you like."

"It's your house, Rob should get the head seat."

"It matters not."

"No, no, it's guest etiquette," George insisted.

George and Clara took the two side seats at the rectangular table, leaving the end seats for the hosts.

Prescilla motioned for everyone to start. "Dig in while everything is nice and hot."

The two couples filled their plates and began to eat.

"My goodness," Clara said. "I don't think I have ever tasted a salad this fresh before."

"We grow all the vegetables ourselves," Prescilla replied.

Silence reigned for a short time while all four were enjoying their meals. Robert spoke next.

"So, how is everyone at the old company?"

George paused for a moment. "Good. They are good."

"Splendid. Nice to know that all is well."

"Tell us, how do you pass the day away now, with no more hustle and bustle of the Big City?"

"Lazily, truth be told. We have our coffee by the lake in the morning. Then I do some gardening until the afternoon gets too hot. I take a nap or read a magazine. We have dinner and then listen to our radio programs in the evening. Nothing too complicated."

"We love our programs too. Clara enjoys the orphan, Beatrice, or Jungle Johnny. I am more partial to Invaders from Space. That Commander Foxx is something else, isn't he?"

"We don't much care for the ones with aliens," Prescilla replied. "Detective Darke is our favorite."

"What? Who doesn't love a good story with aliens and monsters from other worlds?"

"Now, George, stop that. Not everyone enjoys your enthusiasm about aliens from outer space," scolded Clara.

"I did as a young lad," Robert said. "Just, not so much anymore."

"I guess I have never grown out of it," George admitted.

"I just don't seem to have the same interest that I once did."

Robert stared off into space, deep in thought and far from the dinner table. George's voice brought him back again.

"What was all that hubbub about something falling from the sky out this way? It was in all the Big City papers."

"I am not sure what you are referring to."

"How could you not have heard about it?"

"We don't read any of the papers. I have wanted to leave the Big City behind."

"Well, something unexplained apparently fell from the sky and landed out here in the country somewhere. They even had the military out looking but turned up nothing. Enough people had seen it to make the story sound fairly credible. Isn't that right, Clara?"

"It was all over the papers, yes. Just some falling star, if you ask me."

Prescilla shook her head. "We heard nothing about it. But then, as Rob said, we don't read any of the papers and even stay away from the news programs on the radio. Life just seems simpler this way."

"You didn't even notice all the military presence lately?"

"We rarely even leave our own property," Robert replied. "Maybe the odd trip to the grocery store but other than that we have everything that we require right here. Not much reason to leave."

"Well, I envy you guys, there. It would be nice to be able to escape the hectic city life. One day, perhaps, eh, Clara?"

"Yes, dear. That would be nice."

"Are we ready for fresh coffee and dessert?" Prescilla asked, once everyone's plates were empty.

"Sounds good to us," George clapped. "Your banana bread is legendary. Rob used to bring some by the office from time to time and nearly cause a riot from folk fighting for a piece."

Prescilla blushed. "I hope it's as good as you remember."

Prescilla returned from the kitchen, promptly, with a pot of fresh coffee and a tray of her scrumptious banana bread. George wasted no time in attacking the bread. It was as good as he remembered.

The Wainwright's and the King's enjoyed some more small talk during dessert. Afterwards, in the interest of being more comfortable, Prescilla suggested they finish their coffee in the living room.

"That was a fine meal, Prescilla, my compliments to the chef," George said, taking a seat on the sofa.

"Yes it was, indeed," Clara added.

"Thank you, I am glad you all enjoyed it."

"We did. And it was mighty big of you, Rob, to invite us out here like this, after all that mess at the office."

Clara paled. "Now, George, this is not the time for such talk. You'll have to excuse…"

"No, no, Clara. We can't all just sit here and ignore the elephant in the room. Rob and I have been friends from way back, good friends, and it just makes me happy that he was able to look past everything that happened. Warms my heart."

Robert shifted uncomfortably in his chair across from the sofa. "Yes, well, as we get older I think it's silly, and quite frankly unhealthy, to hold onto such grudges. I was pleased you both accepted our invitation."

George nodded. "How could we not when remembering all the good times we had? And look at you both, now. You guys are living this wonderful laid-back life out here. Why, it was probably even a blessing that you had gotten fired. You would have been miserable in the Big City."

Robert smiled, weakly. "You are right. I suppose I should even thank you for the part you played in that. We do enjoy our lives out here."

George stood and walked over to where Robert sat, extending his hand out in a friendly gesture. "Put her there, ole boy. Let bygones be bygones."

Robert accepted and shook his hand. "To old friends. Um, how about we show you around before the sun disappears completely?"

"A splendid idea," Prescilla said. "You both will love the view of the lake. The sunset is beautiful."

"Sounds fantastic," Clara said, just happy to be off that uncomfortable topic of Robert's dismissal at the hands of her husband.

The Wainwright's guided the King's back through the kitchen and out a side door. They walked around to the backyard where the Wainwright's had erected a magnificent garden, but as it was suggested, it was the view of the lake that truly grabbed their attention. The sun was just setting beyond a distant wooded-hill and the water was as calm as could be, like a sheet of glass.

"Good heavens, it's beautiful. Isn't it George?"

He had to agree with his wife. "Indeed, so. I can see why you sit out here every day with a coffee. I must say I am jealous."

The two couples strolled down toward the water's edge, where Robert had built a small dock that extended about fifteen feet out.

"May we?" George asked, motioning to the dock.

"Absolutely. Go see how crystal clear the water is. There is a fairly steep drop off near the end of the dock where the lake gets quite deep."

George and Clara made their way, hand in hand, to the end of wooden dock. It was no lie, they were both quite jealous. They both thought, at the same time, how serene it would be to sit here each day, soaking in this view. George was marveling at how still the water appeared, when he suddenly noticed ripples just below them. Large bubbles were coming up to the surface from some unknown source, deep within the lake.

Clara was the first to notice and gasped out loud. A

hideous tentacle soon broke the surface and writhed about in the air. It was followed by several others and Clara finally screamed with horror, as something large came forth from the water. George was rendered speechless and was paralyzed in place.

The creature was enormous with slimy-green skin and great wings. It possessed a bulbous head with many tentacles where a mouth should be. They wiggled and writhed as if sniffing the air. Giant, milky-white eyes, gazed down at the terrified couple and Clara fainted. With hands, much like a human, it grabbed the King's, who were helpless to resist.

With mouths agape, the Wainwright's watched the spectacle. Nothing could be done to stop this monstrosity that was already old when the Earth was considered young. It spoke, then, in some sickly-gurgling language that was never meant for the ears of humans. The Wainwright's heard this speech in their minds. Despite the indecipherable sound of the language, somehow, Robert and Prescilla knew exactly what it was saying.

"MORE FOOD."

The elder one sunk back beneath surface of the lake, taking the King's with it.

After standing speechless for some time, the Wainwright's turned back toward their house. It was Prescilla that finally broke the silence.

"What happens when we run out of people we don't like?"

Robert looked at his wife but had no answer for that.

"Let's get the table reset. The Wallace's will be here in about an hour."

A DISEASED MIND

Aaron was a troubled soul from the time he was very young. While other young boys took care of their action figures, Aaron pulled his part. He took pleasure in destroying things and imagining their distress, had they been real. His parents hadn't notice anything too out of the ordinary, until they took note of his malice toward animals. Young children generally adored animals and yet Aaron was not among that group. He made an odd request one day, asking if they could get a puppy. His parents, making a wise decision, denied that request, questioning his motives.

So, Aaron just continued to destroy toys in gruesome fashion. Hacking off limbs. Lighting them on fire. Dragging them behind his bicycle while tied to fishing line. The older he got, the more creative his methods became.

In school, he was the quiet kid that kept mostly to himself. The other children found him strange. Nobody could pinpoint one particular thing about him that creeped them out, it was just the general sense of unease they felt in his presence. He appeared to lack emotion. The teachers would gossip with one another about the odd boy. He possessed a cold stare and never smiled, that is until the day they dissected a frog in science class.

Aaron was in his glory, and for the first time, people saw him smile. None would say that it was a warm smile, in fact, the smile only further creeped the others out. While most of the kids found this particular lesson revolting, Aaron obviously enjoyed it, and a little too much.

"Will we be dissecting a human in a future class?" Aaron asked his science teacher.

"Good heavens, no!" his teacher replied, and immediately noticed how truly sad the young boy appeared from the answer.

As a teenager, Aaron was still a recluse. He felt awkward in the presence of others and found it difficult to maintain eye contact. He passed away his free time with monster magazines and watching scary movies at the picture show. Most of the movies he was too young to see, so he found ways to sneak in. Slasher films were his favorite, like, The Red House on the Corner, or The Shadows Have Eyes. He could watch the same films over and over and barely blink an eye. He didn't even purchase popcorn as that was a distraction that took his attention away from the screen. He would sit, motionless, completely transfixed on the film, from start to finish.

His bedroom was adorned with the posters from his favorite films or grisly pictures he cut out of the monster magazines. It brought the boy great joy to be surrounded by such imagery. His mother disapproved but it was not uncommon for kids to be drawn to such movies. The films and magazines were successful for a reason, she figured. There was obviously a market.

As Aaron grew into a young man, he found it increasingly difficult to live at home and get along with his opinionated parents. He managed to secure himself a job in a local butcher's shop, after the butcher found that he had a natural talent for the kind of work required of him. Aaron earned just enough so that he could afford a small one-room apartment above a beer store.

He no longer attended school and when he wasn't working, he was always home. Alone. Aaron still had no friends and family did not visit him. He spent many hours looking out his window, watching drunks come and go from the beer store below. Some of them appeared homeless, purchasing a bottle, or sometimes a case of beer, after they had begged for enough money to do so. Aaron often wondered if anyone would miss them, if they were to suddenly disappear.

His thoughts were becoming darker. His obsession for slasher films became greater. He found himself, more frequently now, imagining those scenes from the movies, playing out before his very eyes. He imagined himself wielding a variety of different weapons with deadly proficiency. He envisioned expressions of fear. Screams of horror. How different would they be, he wondered, when it was real, and not just performed by an actor or actress?

Aaron decided he needed to experience it for himself. Films and magazines were failing to satisfy his hunger. He borrowed a meat cleaver from work one evening and followed a man who exited the beer store, carrying a case under one arm. The man's clothes were ragged and his shoes torn. He looked as though he might live on the streets and therefore would not have anyone waiting for him to return home.

The evening was warm but Aaron wore a long dark jacket, regardless. He kept his head down and followed the man for several blocks, keeping a fair distance between them, so as not to raise suspicion. His heart raced with a mixture of excitement and nervousness. His right hand, which gripped the handle of the cleaver hidden within his pocket, trembled.

Aaron began to quicken his pace, shortening the distance between him and his prey. He smiled at the analogy, that he was now a predator and the man he followed the prey. He was no longer the shy, strange guy, that felt awkward in social situations. Now, he was a hunter. He had a purpose.

His prey turned into an alleyway between two stores which had closed for the night. This was it, Aaron thought, time to make his move. He sped around the corner after the man and then stopped short. His prey had sat down next to two other men who were drinking bottles from brown paper bags. Aaron immediately spun around and headed back the way he had come. He had to abort.

He was overwhelmed with the feeling of disappointment and eyed other people that passed him by, considering a new target. Aaron shook that notion away and returned home. He could not just choose a target out of haste. Hasty decisions could lead to mistakes and he could not afford to make any mistakes.

Aaron lay awake that night, deep in thought. The adrenaline from the hunt was still coursing through his veins. The more he thought about it, the more he realized he had come very close to making a major mistake. If the body of the homeless man had ever been discovered, the police would retrace his steps and look for suspects within that general area. Aaron lived above the beer store that these vagrants frequented, so perhaps this was too close to home. He would need to choose someone further away.

Several days later, Aaron received a letter from his landlord that the cost of his rent would be rising next month. For a brief moment, he considered making his landlord his next target but he quickly realized that was a poor decision. After raising the rent, anyone affected would be prime suspects in the man's disappearance.

Aaron picked up a newspaper that afternoon to browse through the classified section to see if he could find a cheaper place to rent. There were several possible options and he circled a few of interest. He learned that renting a room or a basement in someone else's house was less expensive. The place with the cheapest rent was the farthest away from where he worked, but it was not out of the question. The bus was easy to get to and it would be possible to ride a bicycle if the weather permitted.

That evening, he took a trip out to see the house that was on the far side of town. It was located on a quiet street, a fair distance away from neighbors. It was a small bungalow house that was offering a basement apartment for rent. From Aaron's vantage point, he could see clearly through the front window of the house and observed a couple having dinner. They appeared to be somewhere in their thirties and Aaron found the woman with the long blonde hair to be quite attractive.

Dark thoughts creeped their way into his mind and a

new plan began to formulate. Here was a house far from where he lived, where a couple was allowing random strangers into their home to view the basement. If he was careful about it, there would be no link between Aaron and this couple. The strong desire to become the predator returned and he knew now that he had his new target.

Aaron had the next few days off work, so he went back to the house early the next morning, finding a good spot to watch and remain out of sight. He thought it best to study any routines this couple might have. He observed the man leave the house at 8am with a briefcase and get into a car, no doubt to head off to work. The woman remained home for the entire day and the man returned at 5pm. The next day was the same routine as the first. On the third day, the woman left for two hours and returned with grocery bags, but that was the only deviation.

Now, Aaron was thinking to move on the woman when she was alone during the day. He could pose as a potential renter to gain access to the house. As long as he was careful that nobody noticed him come and go, or leave any clues behind, he could be in the clear. There would be no link to make him a suspect. In fact, in most cases involving a missing or murdered wife, the husband was always the prime suspect.

Due to his work schedule, Aaron returned to the house the following week and was satisfied to observe the same routine. He picked up a newspaper to confirm that the basement was still listed for rent and it was. He decided that Wednesday would be the day.

He would sleep not a wink that Tuesday night. His level of excitement was off the charts. He worked through a variety of scenarios while he replayed many of his favorite movie scenes in his mind. This would be the first adventure of many, he thought. He wondered if others before him had thought of the idea of posing as a potential renter. It was the perfect way in.

That Wednesday morning, Aaron packed a bag with the things that he thought would be essential. Meat cleaver. Gloves. Duct tape. Garbage bags. Change of clothes. Scissors. A container of bleach. He pulled on an old pair of boots and wore his long black jacket. He got off the bus several blocks from his destination and walked the remainder of the way. It was fairly early in the morning and Aaron saw very few people up and about.

He found his way to the desired street without incident and took up watch from his usual hiding place behind a tree. No neighbors had seen his approach, as far as he was aware. It didn't take long before he was watching the man of the house pull out of the driveway in his car and head off to work. Aaron smiled a wicked smile. It was time.

He steeled his nerve and approached the house, ever mindful of any neighbors. There was none. He took a deep breath and knocked on the front door. His heart beat so rapidly that it threatened to leap out of his chest. When there was no immediate response, he knocked again.

Aaron was finally rewarded when the woman of the house opened the door. She appeared surprised that someone would be here this early in the morning.

"Yes? Can I help you?"

"Um, good m-morning to you. I am here about the ad you placed for your basement apartment."

Aaron always found interacting with others to be an awkward thing and he shifted from foot to foot and could not look the woman in the eyes. He could sense that she felt uneasy.

"Our ad said evening appointments only. My husband will…"

Aaron cut her off. "I am sorry I did see that, but I work evenings all this week and that would be impossible."

"Perhaps, you could come back next week?"

"I really need to find a place this week. I have to leave my current place by this weekend, so I am really in a jam here."

"My husband usually handles these things."

"That's alright, I just need to take a quick look at the basement and then I could call him later to discuss the details. I just need five minutes of your time, that's all. Just a quick peek."

"Well, I suppose that would be alright."

"Thank you so much, I really appreciate this. I need a place as soon as possible and your house is the perfect location for me with regards to work."

She nodded. "Come in."

The woman closed the door behind them and Aaron found it difficult to breathe. His hands, which he kept buried in his coat pockets, trembled with nervousness. He dared not remove them from his pockets, as he didn't wish to touch anything accidently, until he could put his gloves on.

His legs trembled and he did his best to appear that nothing was out of sorts, as she motioned for him to follow her over to the basement door.

"There is a separate entrance at the side of the house," she said. "But we will just use this one."

The inside of the house smelled sweet. Something

delicious was baking in the oven. The living room they passed through was spotless and elegantly decorated. Aaron tried not to get distracted by his surroundings and focused on the attractive woman he followed. She opened the door that led to the basement and flicked on a light.

She went first, down the narrow stairwell, with Aaron closely behind. The perfume she wore was intoxicating. They passed the side door and then descended further to the basement. The woman flicked another light switch and Aaron could now see two doors. He tightly gripped the handle of the meat cleaver which was concealed in his deep right pocket. The woman opened the door on the left and motioned for Aaron to take a peek.

"It is a small room, but tell me what you think. There is another switch just inside on your left."

Aaron still had not put his gloves on, so he carefully used one of his knuckles to flick the light switch to illuminate the room. What he saw in the room puzzled him.

"Ah, what is all this?"

Something struck the back of Aaron's head hard and the floor rushed upward to meet his face. When he opened his eyes, he could not tell how much time had passed. Every slight movement sent a sharp, searing pain, throughout his head. He came to realize that he was in a standing position and shackled to the wall of that small room. His vision was blurry but he could make out two people standing in front of him. As his eyes slowly came into focus, he recognized the man and woman who owned the house.

"He is awake?" she asked.

The man was holding Aaron's bag and was looking

through its contents. "And just what were you planning to do with all this stuff, young man?"

Aaron couldn't muster the where-with-all to respond.

The man smiled, evilly. "I have a feeling I know exactly what you were planning. So I am willing to bet that nobody knew you were coming here today. I am also willing to bet that you were careful that nobody saw you enter our house. That tells me that nobody will be looking for you here when someone realizes that you are missing."

The woman produced a kitchen knife and matched her husband's evil smile. "We have all the time in the world to have fun with this one."

CREEP'S MOTEL

The rain was coming down with a vengeance. The windshield wipers were barely able to keep up, making visibility nearly non-existent. Gordon could see very little of the road ahead and his wife Martha was now in a state of panic.

"You can't even see the road. I think we need to stop."

"Stop where, Martha? I can't just stop, this is a highway. You want some truck to come up from behind and run right over us?"

"Well, pull off the road at least. I didn't mean to stop right here in the middle."

Their weekend trip from the Big City to Shallow Lake had gone horribly awry. What should have only been a two-hour drive was now four, and they felt they were no closer to their destination than they were two hours earlier.

"I told you that road didn't look right back there. You

should have just kept going straight."

"Well, the directions said to make a left off of Highway Nine."

"Yes, but it said to make a left onto Kingsway. That road you took didn't say Kingsway and I think that turn came a lot sooner than it should have."

"I was told the first left was Kingsway. The sign must have come down in this storm, perhaps. That should have been the correct turn."

"Obviously it wasn't."

Thunder cracked overhead and it was so loud that Gordon nearly veered right off the road. Martha shrieked.

"Alright, we really need to stop somewhere," she implored. "Where do you think we are?"

"I haven't seen a sign in hours. I was thinking we should be near Bridgeway Township but none of this looks familiar to me."

"I haven't even seen a street light or a gas bar in over an hour. Please, we need to stop at the next one we see."

"At this point, I will gladly stop at the next gas bar. We are going to run out of a fuel if we don't find one soon."

Martha's face turned a whiter shade of pale, if that was even possible. "Oh, Gordon, why didn't you fill up before we left?"

"It should have only been a two-hour drive. We had enough for that. Look, there is another road up here on the left."

"Can you see a sign? What road is it?"

"I can't see a sign at all. I think we should take it, though."

"No, Gordon, no more side roads. Let's just stay on

this main highway."

"But maybe we could find some houses and ask someone where we are."

"It's almost midnight. You think we are just going to go knock on some stranger's door in this kind of weather? Who in their right mind would answer? Just stay on this road and we are bound to come across something soon."

"Fine."

Gordon gripped the steering wheel so tightly his knuckles were white. He had never driven in such a storm before. Lightning arced across the sky and momentarily lit up the road ahead, as if it were the middle of day. Both their hearts sunk at the sight before them.

"Did you see that, Martha? The bridge is completely flooded."

Martha sighed. "I suppose we will have to go back to that last turnoff then."

"Maybe if I get a good run at it, we can make it across the bridge."

Martha appeared mortified. "You will do no such thing! The last thing we need right now is for our car to sink in there! Gordon, turn around."

"Fine."

Gordon doubled back and turned down the nameless side road. They were in a heavily-wooded area which made everything appear that much darker. The road was not paved and his new worry was getting stuck in the mud, though, he did not voice that aloud. Martha was already in such a frenzy that one more thing could send her completely over the edge. He also thought it best not to mention that the needle on the fuel indicator was now in the red. That was a major concern.

Twenty minutes later, the woods thinned and the road came to a four-way intersection. Gordon and Martha both smiled and allowed themselves a moment to laugh at their sudden good fortune. On the far side of the intersection, they spotted a motel. The neon vacancy sign was on, though, two of the letters were burnt out. And to put the couple in an even better mood, there was a gas pump at the motel.

"Someone is looking out for us," Martha said, jubilantly.

Gordon exhaled, the timing could not have been better. He turned in to the empty parking lot and another flash of lightning lit up the night sky.

"Oh, good heavens," Martha said. "Did you see that sign?"

Gordon had. "Creep's Motel? Who would name a motel that?"

"That's absurd. I don't see any other cars here. Strange for a Friday night."

Gordon was just thinking the same thing. But then, they did not even know where here was. Another thing they both noticed was the state of the motel. To suggest it would need some fixing up would be an understatement. It was a long, single-level building, with what appeared to be ten rooms and a main office. The only visible light came from within the office.

Gordon parked the car in front of the first room, which was adjacent to the office. His headlights revealed a broken window and a door that did not sit properly on its hinges.

Worry crept back into Martha's mind. "Ah, I don't think I like the look of this place. It has the right title because it gives me the creeps."

"Don't be so silly. A lot of the old motels out in the middle of nowhere are like this. This storm is just making it appear creepier than I am sure it really is."

"I don't know. I think it would look just as creepy in the middle of the day. How about you just get some gas and find out where we are, then we can leave."

"Martha, I am exhausted and this storm is horrendous. We are going to need to wait somewhere for it to clear up."

"Not here."

"Nonsense. A place like this will probably cost next to nothing for a room. I can see someone in the office. Are you coming in with me?"

Martha reluctantly nodded. She had no real desire to get out of the car but they had been driving so long she figured she should at least use the restroom while they were here. The pair ran the short distance from their car to the office and still arrived inside, soaking wet. It was as if they had both just jumped fully-clothed into a pool.

Chimes jingled on the door and startled the middle-aged man, who moments before, had been asleep behind the front counter.

"Oh my, where did you folk come from?" he asked, rubbing his eyes.

"That's a long story, my friend. First we need to know where we are," Gordon replied.

"The middle of nowhere," the man joked.

Gordon was not in the mood. "We are from the Big City and we're trying to get to Shallow Lake. How far are we from the lake?"

"Shallow Lake? Hmm," he scratched his chin in

thought. "I don't reckon I have ever heard of Shallow Lake."

"Never heard of...oh never mind. What town are we in?"

"Oldhill."

"Oldhill? I have no idea where Oldhill is. How far away are we from the Big City?"

"Oh, I would say purdy far."

Gordon was finding it difficult to keep his eyes from the man's stained shirt. His grubby appearance was a distraction. The office was in disarray and layers of dust lined every surface. Perhaps Martha was right, Gordon thought.

"Look, maybe we could just get some gas and a map, and then we will be on our way?"

"Our pump is empty."

"What?"

"Hasn't been used in years."

Gordon noticed his wife tense up as she realized they were not going to be going anywhere, anytime soon.

"Joe? Who are ya talking to?" a woman said, as she entered the office from a back room. "Oh, howdy folks."

The woman's hair was disheveled and she had an equally as grubby appearance as the man behind the counter. She was picking at the remnants of a recent meal from her teeth with a toothpick.

"This is my wife, Maude. Maude, these folk just arrived from that wicked storm."

"Ah, be needin a room, will ya?"

"Well, we were just hoping to get some gas and directions and be on our way."

"Our pump is empty," the woman restated.

"Yeah, we just heard that grim news."

"So, ya best be bringin yer bags in. Ya got the pick of any room ya like. The storm should clear come mornin, don't ya be thinkin, Joe?"

"I reckon so, Maude."

"Got some leftovers in the back room here that's still warm. Once ya get settled I can bring some to yer room."

Martha paled. She could not imagine the state of the kitchen in this place. "That won't be necessary, we had a big dinner before we left and had some snacks in the car."

"Suit yerself."

"Since you are kinda in a jam, with the storm and all, I will even offer you our best room for regular price," Joe smiled.

"Ah, much appreciated. I suppose I will go grab our bags from the car."

Martha grabbed Gordon's arm tightly. "I am coming with you, I, ah, forgot something."

"Nonsense, Junior can fetch your bags. Maude, go wake Junior."

"Oh, no, no. No need to wake anyone. We are fine," Gordon insisted.

Before heading back out into the rain, Gordon turned, with a burning question on his mind.

"Just curious, what's with the name of your place? Creep's Motel? Really? Are you trying to keep people away?"

Both Joe and Maude bristled at the comment. "Well, that is our name. We are Joe and Maude Creep."

Martha pinched Gordon's arm to the point where it hurt and then dragged him out the front door. The rain had not let up one bit so they both ran as fast as they could back to the car. Once inside, Martha whirled on her husband.

"As if the Creep's weren't creepy enough, you had to go and insult them!"

"How could I know that was their name? Who has the name, Creep?"

"They do!"

"Suits them, too."

"We are not staying here tonight."

"What? We have no choice."

"I cannot sleep in this place. I have a very bad feeling. They give me the heebie jeebies."

"Well, we have no gas and have no idea where we are. Not to mention this storm."

"Didn't you say once that you drove a half hour with the gas needle on red?"

"Yes, but we have already been driving with it in the red. We won't get very far."

"I don't care, anywhere is better than here."

"You say that now. You will change your mind when we are sleeping in the car out on some dark road somewhere."

"No I won't."

"Dear, be reasonable. It's not safe for us out there. Now, we have to stay here tonight and then we can assess things in the morning. Hopefully the storm will stop by then. We found this place so I am sure there is somewhere else close by where we can get gas, but we can't just go driving blindly in the dark."

"My gut tells me something is off about this place."

"Don't be silly. It's dark, it's stormy, and the owners are a touch creepy. You are letting your imagination run wild."

Suddenly, Martha screamed at the top of her lungs, which caused Gordon to shriek as well, though, he was not quite sure why. His wife had been looking behind him, so he turned and shrieked a second time at the sight of a face pressed against the glass of the car window.

"I got the key to your room," Joe said, from within the hood of his raincoat. "It's right over here if you want to follow me with your bags."

It took several moments before the couple got their breathing back under control. Martha gave her husband a glare that told him she did not want to get back out of the car but they really were not presented much of a choice.

"Come on, it will only be a few more hours until morning, then we'll leave. I'll grab the bags from the trunk. Let's go."

Gordon grabbed three bags and they both ran for the cover of the motel's awning, and then followed Joe down to room 105. Gordon was pleased that at least this room's window was intact and the door sat properly on its hinges.

Joe unlocked the door and invited the couple to follow him inside. The room was quite dark, so the couple hesitated by the doorway until their escort had entered and turned on a small lamp next to the double bed. This was their best room? Gordon and Martha thought silently in unison.

"Is there anything else you need?" their host asked.

"I think we will be fine, thanks," Gordon answered.

"Once you get settled, you can drop by the office and get things squared away. We accept cash and charge cards."

Gordon nodded and closed the door quickly behind

the departing Joe Creep. He turned back and surveyed the room again. Dust covered every surface within the small nondescript room and the awful choice in wallpaper was peeling in several places. There was one double bed, a side table with the lamp, and a writing desk under the window, next to the front door. A tiny bathroom was located at the back of the room and there was a door that linked this room with the one on the left, which was typical in some places. A horrible painting of a family standing in front of a farm hung crookedly on one of the walls. It looked as though a child had painted it with their fingers.

Martha inspected the bed and wrinkled her nose in disgust. "The sheets are all stained. I can't stay here."

"We have no choice, I already told you. We can sleep on the floor, if you prefer. We can pretend we are camping."

Martha was in no mood for jokes.

"I am going to go pay, so you get comfortable."

Thunder cracked outside and caused Martha to jump in fright. "Don't leave me in this room alone."

"I will just be a minute. Lock the door behind me if you like. And stop worrying."

Gordon left and Martha did indeed lock the deadbolt. Her heart was racing a million miles a minute. She had not been exaggerating in the least when she said her gut told her something was off about this place. It was just a nagging feeling that would not let up or allow her to relax.

She walked about the room, conducting a thorough inspection. Even the carpet was stained, she noticed with disgust. Martha stopped in front of the ugly painting and something odd immediately drew her attention. Three people stood in front of a farm, and one of them had a hole for an eye. An actual hole through the painting. Curious, Martha pulled the painting off the wall and her stomach did more flip flops as she found there was a small round hole in the wall. The perfect peep hole, she figured, from the room next door.

She quickly retrieved a tissue from her purse and stuffed it in the dark hole. Goosebumps ran up and down her neck and arms. She glanced at the door that connected the two rooms and her heart skipped a beat at her discovery. There was no lock. She carefully tried the door knob and found that door was indeed locked, but from the other side.

A knock on the front door nearly had Martha jumping straight through the roof of the room. Once she recovered, she quickly unlocked the door and pulled it open.

"Gordon, I nearly…," Martha's sentence was interrupted by another scream.

It was not Gordon who was standing outside the door, but a very large person whose face was concealed behind the hood of a raincoat. Martha was frozen in place with fear.

"W-who are y-you?" she managed to ask.

No answer.

"My husband will be b-back any m-moment now."

No answer.

"P-please don't h-hurt me."

"Junior! You get away from there now. Stop scaring the nice lady!" Joe shouted from outside.

Martha breathed a giant sigh of relief when the silent individual walked away and Gordon came back into the room.

Joe stuck his head around the doorway. "I apologize, Miss. Junior was just curious to see the new guests, is all."

"He doesn't say much, does he?"

"Junior is a simple lad. Well, goodnight folks. Give a holler if you need anything."

Once the door was closed again, Gordon noticed the frantic look on Martha's face.

"I am not staying here tonight," she stated, with a quiver in her voice.

"What? I just paid."

"We are leaving."

"The man apologized for his son. He didn't mean to scare you, you heard him, he is just simple."

"It's not just that, Gordon, come here. I found a peep hole in the wall. It was disguised with the painting."

"You are jumping to conclusions."

"Am I? What about this door that connects to the next room? It's only locked from the other side. Anyone could come in here from the other room."

"Oh, stop it. Come in here for what purpose?"

"To murder us in our sleep!"

"Do you realize how ridiculous you sound? You watch too many of those late night movies."

"Something doesn't feel right. These Creeps are real creeps."

"It's just their name! You are letting this storm affect your judgment. This is all in your mind. Granted, the room could be a little better but…"

"A little better?"

"Fine, the room is a dump. The whole place is a dump. But we are stuck here, just for tonight."

"I refuse to stay here. We are leaving."

"But, dear! We won't get far before we run out of gas!"

"We will be away from here and that's all that matters."

"Oh for Pete's sake!"

*   *   *   *

Maude rushed into the main office and the sound of her shuffling slippers jolted her husband awake, who had just nodded off behind the counter again.

"I thought I heard something," she said. "Joe, that young couple just drove off."

"Eh?"

"That couple. They just left."

Joe joined his wife by the front window and caught a glimpse of tail lights just before they faded from view.

"Hmm, you're right."

"Dang it! I bet Junior plum scared them off. I told ya that ya should hit that one in the head with the shovel when he was in here payin."

"Now, Maude, you know I prefer to get them in their sleep."

"Maybe we ought to send Junior after them? They might not get far with little gas."

"We don't want Junior catching a cold, it's miserable out there."

"Well, there ain't much left from that last couple. Ya want us to starve?"

"Don't forget we still have that traveling salesman in the cold storage."

EYES THAT FOLLOW

From my vantage point, I had the entire library in view. Although the room was quite large, there was nothing that could escape my notice. At this moment, I was observing a secret meeting between Davral, the resident sorcerer, and Lucia, the Queen's sister.

Davral was a sly and meddlesome man. He was afforded much freedom here in the castle, as the King trusted him, foolishly. The man was an outsider and dabbled in dark magic. I believe nobody, save myself, knew just how dark. I was only aware of the sorcerer's less-than-desirable studies and secret meetings through spying. I was an adept spy and gathering secrets was my specialty.

I was born right here in this very castle and have lived all of my twenty-three years here. Make no mistake, though, I am not royalty or nobility. I am still only a commoner. Both of my parents worked here at the castle.

My mother was a chambermaid and did laundry and made beds. My father, before his untimely death from disease, swept the hallways and cleaned windows. From a very young age, I took after my father and wielded a broom as soon as I was able to lift one. Since that time, I have added window cleaning and a little gardening to my daily duties.

While life inside the castle was much better than life anywhere else in the realm, I was still only a commoner and I was paid and treated as such. I wasn't happy with my lot in life. I wanted more. Most castle workers dreamed of one day becoming a steward and being in charge of all the other workers. While that did pay more, and offer a tad more prestige, it still wouldn't satisfy my desires. I wanted to be rich like the lords and ladies that frequented the halls of this castle. I craved gold and all the things that it could buy.

Having lived in this castle for my entire life, I had become quite familiar with every corner. I was trusted and granted access to many rooms that were off-limits to most. I studied the complete layout of the immense building and learned of all the secret passages and corridors. The castle was riddled with them. Some were common knowledge and others, as I discovered with layers of thick dust, were only known by me. The castle was built hundreds of years before the current ruling King and Queen, so the architect, and those that commissioned these secret passages, were all but dust in the wind.

Years ago, while exploring these hidden ways quite often, I was able to unearth many secrets. Not secrets of the castle, itself, but secrets about its residents. Shady dealings. Torrid affairs. Nefarious plots. The kinds of things that people would pay to find out. And pay in gold.

Lots of gold.

I hid in corridors, out of sight. I spied with peep holes, or merely listened through walls. I gathered information that was never meant for ears outside the appointed meeting rooms. At first, I cleverly sold my secrets anonymously, through letters, requiring payments to be left in secluded locations. I was fearful of retribution. Later, as I amassed greater amounts of information, I dealt with a select few people in person. To some people, I was too valuable an asset to lose, to others, I was too dangerous a person to dare inflict harm upon. To cross me, was to find all your secrets laid bare, for all to see. Some people paid me for secrets. Others paid me to keep their secrets. Business was good.

I was becoming so good that I had caught the attention of the royal spymaster; the man who was charged with protecting the King from plots against his life. This was a deadly man, full of resources at his disposal, and unlimited coins to see his job was done well. And it was this very man who quite often would enlist my aid. He allowed me to keep my own secrets as to how I obtained the knowledge that I did. Although, I truly believed that he already knew, but crawling through dusty passages was beneath him. He let me do the dirty work but compensated me handsomely for my efforts.

The spymaster was becoming increasingly suspicious of Davral and had tasked me to keep an eye on the sorcerer. It was an impossible task when the man was inside his own private chamber. There was no way to get eyes and ears in there at all. Fortunately, for me, he spent much of his time in the castle's library. The library was seldom used by others and made a great place for the sorcerer's dark studies and secret meetings.

Davral was not the only one who used the library for reasons other than reading. There was the time I observed one of the castle's guards writing a letter to an acquaintance on the outside, which contained details of the castle's layout. That man was later hung for treason. I had also observed several rendezvous between Lord Brass and Lady Gwendolyn. The problem there was that each was married to someone different. Lord Brass was beheaded and Lady Gwendolyn was publically flogged for their indiscretions. There was also the former steward of the castle, who would use a corner of the library to sleep most of the day away, while he was paid to be working. He was stripped of his job and exiled from the realm.

Davral was up to something but I had yet to uncover what it was. He spent long hours poring over the pages of dark texts, researching such awful topics as demonology and necromancy. He appeared to be most interested in the summoning of demons to extract information on the casting of certain spells. It was said the sorcerer wielded terrible power. I had never witnessed any, firsthand, but the tales were many of the unfortunate fools who ended up on the wrong end of one of Davral's spells. He was a master of transmutation and had a particular love of transforming people into other things.

Spying on the sorcerer was not a job I took lightly. He was a guarded and paranoid individual on the best of days. Most people with secrets generally were. If it wasn't for my knowledge of hidden passageways, I would never have even gotten close to the man. Most often, I made a note of which books he read in the library and where he returned them to on the shelf. Afterwards, when he was gone and I deemed it safe to do so, I would creep in from my hiding place to locate the books.

Just recently, he had spent nearly two hours reading through an old tome of poisons, which contained many home-brewed recipes of deadly concoctions. That raised red flags in my mind. I felt that this was something that the spymaster would need to know. Was Davral plotting to poison someone? The King, perhaps? So engrossed in thought was I that day, that I had not even noticed that Davral had returned to the library and stood directly behind me.

Now, I looked down on Davral and Lucia, who were seated in a shadowed-corner of the library. They were speaking in hushed tones but my acute hearing picked up most of the details. The rest I pieced together from my years of reading lips. The spymaster's greatest fears were confirmed; Davral was plotting against the King, and with the Queen's own sister, no less. The sorcerer had somehow enlisted the aid of Lucia, who planned to administer a lethal dose of poison into the drinks of the King and Queen. Davral had manufactured the concoction in his private laboratory and now it was Lucia's job to get it into the hands of the royal couple. This was the greatest secret that I had ever uncovered, but nobody would ever learn of it.

Davral and Lucia concluded their private discussion and walked in my direction. Lucia kept eyeing my location, suspiciously, until she approached for a closer look. The sorcerer joined her with a smug smile upon his bearded-face.

"I have never noticed that painting before," she said.

"I believe it is a recent acquisition," Davral replied.

"I could swear those eyes moved. I felt like they have been following me around this room."

"Merely an illusion created by the talented artist, no doubt."

"That man's face looks vaguely familiar. Wait, it resembles that man that sweeps the halls. Don't you think?"

"I can definitely see the similarities but who would waste their time painting the portrait of a commoner and floor sweeper? Just a strange coincidence."

"I suppose. I haven't seen him around lately either. Would be amusing to have him stand here and compare the two faces."

"Amusing, indeed. I heard the man has run away. I don't think we shall ever see him around again."

"Ah, well."

Lucia turned and exited the library leaving me alone with the vile sorcerer.

"You like to spy on people in the library," he stated. "Now you can hang there as a painting for an eternity and spy all you want."

His cruel laughter echoed throughout the room.

PENPALS

May 5

Dear Mr. Baxter,

I found the ad that you placed in our local paper seeking a pen pal. It wasn't an easy thing to spot, due to the fact that it was quite small and tucked underneath the giant ad for that sleazy auto dealer. But I am someone with a lot of time on my hands and I do read the entire paper, word for word, from cover to cover. I must admit, I lead a rather dull life and reading the morning paper is one of my favorite things to look forward to each day. Sad I know. So I can see by your mailing address that you are not very close to the Big City. About three hours by train, I believe. I am curious to know why you chose our paper here to post your ad? I suppose I should refrain from rambling on too much in my first correspondence, as I may not even be of much interest to you to elicit a reply. If you do, however, care to respond, I will write more the next time, I promise.

Yours truly,

Margaret

*   *   *   *

May 19

Dear Margaret,

It was splendid to receive your letter in the post. Yours is the first reply I have ever gotten, and to be completely honest, I wasn't holding out much hope of hearing from anyone. I was unable to see where my ad was placed in your paper but someone found it at least, so it worked. Why you ask, did I choose your paper for my ad? Simply put, the Big City is far from my home. It is something different. I live in a very small town where everyone knows everyone. So the chances would be great that somebody responding to an ad near me, would most likely be someone I am already familiar with. There is not much thrill in corresponding with someone I already know. In addition to that, there are so many people in the Big City, that the odds were greater that someone would reply, and someone did. As stated in my ad, I am quite a lonely person and was seeking someone to converse with on a regular basis. Don't you enjoy the thrill of expecting something in the post? And then reveling in that joyous feeling you get when you notice that the postman has brought it for you? Admittedly, I was not expecting a reply, so my feeling of joy at noticing your letter in my box was that much greater. My hands were even shaking as I opened the envelope. Silly I know. I live in a very small house in a thickly-wooded area. One might even consider it just a cabin. I look after my ailing mother, who is bed-ridden, and she is the only other person I really speak with. Unfortunately, she contracted the disease a year ago and her health has been on a steady decline. Most days now, she does not even have the energy to entertain a meaningful conversation. Speaking of which, I should cut this letter short and check on Mother. You were silly to say that I may not find you interesting enough to elicit a response. I look forward to hearing from you again and learning a little more about you.

Your friend,
Donald Baxter

*   *   *   *

May 31

Dear Mr. Baxter,
It was lovely to hear back from you. I completely agree with you about the thrilling feeling of expecting something to arrive in the post. I know we have only just begun to converse but I found myself eagerly checking my box each morning to see if you had sent a reply. The feeling is foreign to me, as until now, all I expect to receive are my monthly bills. This is surely a welcomed change. I am terribly sorry to hear about your mother. It is good to know that she has someone there to care for her. Are you close to town? Close to your neighbors? How old are you, if I may ask? So a little bit about myself. I am in my mid-

forties and I live alone. I was an only child and both my parents passed several years ago. I was left with a large chunk of money as an inheritance so I currently do not work. I will be honest with you, I suffer from anxiety when around too many people, and sometimes find it difficult to leave my apartment. Once I had enough money to do so, I had to leave my suffocating place of work. I do not do much these days, and like yourself, find that I am very lonely. I read the paper in the morning. I water and talk to my plants. Some days I will take walks in a fairly-empty park near to my apartment. I read books. My evenings are generally spent listening to various radio programs, which I thoroughly enjoy. Then I sleep and repeat the whole process anew in the morning. Exciting isn't it? Well, today is looking like a very sunny day, so I suppose I may attempt to get out for a walk and some fresh air. Wish your mother well for me and write back whenever you have time.

Yours truly,
Margaret

*   *   *   *

June 12

Dear Margaret,
Hello again, my new friend. Please, call me Donald. Mr. Baxter sounds far too formal. We are also not that distant in age, as I am closing in on forty-eight. I appreciate your concern and your warm wishes for Mother. Sadly, she has not been showing any signs of improvement and has

spoken very little of late. So believe me, your letters are a wonderful distraction. They come at a time when I need them the most. My neighbors are not very close at all. My house is somewhat secluded, located at the end of a bumpy dirt road. The forest is thick around me and a babbling brook provides a pleasant soundtrack. I don't own a motor vehicle but it is about a twenty-minute bike ride into town. It feels like it's been ages since I have been in town and socialized with anyone. Unfortunately, I do not own a radio either. This house is very old and there is no electricity, so you'll have to pardon me, but I am unfamiliar with your radio programs. What do you like so much about them? You seem to be a charming woman, have you never married before? Pardon me, if that is getting too personal. You may ignore that question if you wish. I can hear my soup boiling on the woodstove so I will end this letter now. I hope you enjoyed your walk in the park that day and each time since then. I eagerly anticipate your next reply.

Your friend,
Donald Baxter

*   *   *   *

June 23

Dear Donald,
How is your mother doing? How are you coping? I will just say that seeing your letter in my box this morning brought a huge smile to my face. Our correspondence has now become part of my routine and sometimes I check my

box several times a day. The postman is usually here by noon, but sometimes I imagine that he might arrive earlier, so I find myself repeatedly checking. So, no electricity? I admire you living the simple life, however, I do so enjoy my radio programs. Little Orphan Beatrice and Detective Darke are my favorites. I listen to them religiously each week, and while fictional, I feel their lives have become a part of my own. I cannot wait to hear what happens in each episode. They give me something to look forward to, much like your letters, now. And to answer your question, no I have never been married. I have never found someone compatible. Oh, I have to mention that the other day, I found myself looking into the price of train tickets to your town. The trip would be reasonably inexpensive. What do you think about meeting for lunch and a coffee one afternoon this summer? I think it would be wonderful to put a face to the letters. Let me know your thoughts, and I look forward to your reply.

Yours truly,
Margaret

*   *   *   *

July 2

Dear Margaret,
I have been coping well, thank you for inquiring. Mother is the same, I regret to say. I, too, thoroughly enjoy receiving your letters and honestly it is the only thing I look forward to. I don't have much else going on in my life and as I

stated before, I don't have electricity in order to enjoy your radio programs. Though, they do sound quite interesting. Your idea does sound splendid but I feel it is just too far for you to travel. Three hours, one way, just for lunch? Then there is the issue of Mother. I shouldn't really leave her for very long. Perhaps, some other time in the future? In the meantime, I could describe myself, to give you an idea of who you have been conversing with. I am a few inches short of the six feet mark. I have salt and pepper hair, with a beard to match. Blue eyes. Let's see, what else? Oh, I am possibly a little heavier now than I should be, given my sedimentary lifestyle these last few years. Does that help? How has the weather been over there? Have you been enjoying your walks?

Your friend,
Donald

*   *   *   *

July 15

Dear Donald,
I hope you are well. I have been enjoying my walks when the weather allows for it. It has been raining a lot this year, though. Well, I did something really spontaneous yesterday. I understand your concerns about your Mother and the travel time I would need to endure to visit you, but I went ahead and purchased a train ticket. I can read a book on the train so that does not bother me in the least. And I was thinking I could just visit your house. I would very much like to bring your Mother some flowers. I

wouldn't have to stay long at all. The idea is that could we meet face to face. I really hope you won't mind this, terribly. My ticket is for July 29. I timed it so that you should have already received this letter and will be aware of my impending arrival. I should reach the train station in your town by approximately noon. From there I can hire a motor car to take me to your place. I will bring the coffee. I have to say I am very excited. It's been so very long since I have ventured outside the Big City. I will keep this letter short, seeing as how we will converse in person quite soon. Looking forward to meeting you, Donald.

Yours truly,
Margaret

*   *   *   *

September 21

Dear Margaret,
First of all, allow me to apologize for everything. This has taken me longer to send than I had planned, but I wasn't sure how best to explain this. I feel terrible that you had to waste your time traveling here and I know you must have a million questions running through your mind. I truly hope that you did not hurt yourself when you fell, running from the cabin. It was wonderful for me to see you in person, it really was. You are even prettier than I had dared to imagine. I am sorry that you cannot say the same, as you were unable to see me. Oh, dear, where do I begin? I have been dead for a long time, Margaret, longer than I can even recall. Shortly after Mother had passed, loneliness and

despair got the better of me, and in a moment of weakness, I took my own life. But that wasn't the end for me, no, not at all. I am not sure if this was a punishment handed down by God, or perhaps even the Devil himself, but I was cursed to continue to live in this cabin, alone. No, not live, sorry, I should rephrase that. I have been cursed to exist, somehow, within this cabin. I cannot leave and I cannot be seen by anyone. Margaret, I am so dreadfully lonely. Were I able to end this existence in some way, I would have, long before now. I did discover that for some reason, I am able to manipulate small items, such as a pencil and paper. The post office believes that someone still lives here, and continues to drop off and pick up mail from my front door. I watched you enter my cabin that day, Margaret. I saw the confusion etched into your face as you looked around. Nobody has dusted in here in so long, I apologize for the state of the place. I wanted so badly to communicate with you, to let you know that I was here. I did the only thing that I could and began to write, "Hello Margaret," on the piece of paper sitting on the dinner table. I realize how startling that must have been to witness. I didn't mean to frighten you so. I wished you had not run away so quickly. I wished you could have stayed longer so I could have written you an explanation. Please, Margaret, can we not remain friends? I am so lonely.

THE MOLE PEOPLE

I awoke with such delighted excitement. The blazing sun that sent forth its warm rays through my bedroom window, confirmed that it was indeed morning. I thought the morning would never come. The previous night, I tossed and turned, with little hope of falling asleep and speeding up the coming of the dawn.

I had waited for this day for so long that when I climbed into bed, my mind would not allow sleep to come. I spent the first hour just imagining what it will be like to gaze upon real mole people for the first time. I had seen drawings in school, of course, but nothing could compare to seeing one of these elusive creatures in the flesh.

My cousin Stew claims to have seen one years ago, over by the Bubbling Falls. Nobody believes him, least of all me. Stew was a practical joker and apt to make up grand tales. I had fallen prey to his tomfoolery enough that I was almost certain he had never seen one of the mole people.

He could tell a convincing tale, I will give him that, but his past deceits were proof enough for my dismissal of his claim.

As Stew did not count, I did not know anyone personally who had seen a real mole person. They lived far underground, and the rare times that they did come to the surface, it was only at night. Their sensitive eyes could not handle the brightness of the sun, plus, the night allowed them the cover they required to sneak into towns in order to steal food and supplies. My town had been the victim of several raids by the mole people over the years, but it was not until recently, that one had ever been captured.

That mole person, a male it was said, was sold to the traveling carnival so that he could be put on display. While a proper habitat was being built, a second mole person was captured. Now, the carnival has two mole people and today is the first day that they will be on display to the public. There is a nominal fee involved with the pleasure of viewing them but I have been saving money for weeks now in jubilant anticipation of this day.

Even my brother, Ed, had trouble sleeping as his excitement nearly equaled my own. Generally, his snoring, or just heavy breathing, kept me awake at night but this last night he was silent. The few times I glanced in his direction, I saw his eyes wide open, much like mine.

We were typical brothers, in that we tended to annoy each other quite often and rarely could get along. But this day we had something in common. We were both dying to get our first peek at the mole people. Mother called us for breakfast and we made our way down to the kitchen.

"Are you both excited this morning?" Mother asked.

We both nodded in unison as we began to wolf down

our cereal. She taught us not to speak with our mouths full but we didn't need to, she could read the answer clearly on our faces.

"Your father has gone to fuel up and then will be back to pick you both up to take you to the carnival."

"Aren't you coming with us?" I asked.

"Oh, no, I don't think I need to see any mole people. Dreadful creatures they are."

"You mean you are not even curious to see a real one? Not at all?" my brother wondered.

"Not at all. You know, when I was a little girl, we had a farm over in the Barren Plains. The mole people would raid our farm at night, from time to time, and steal everything we had to eat."

"And you never saw one? Ever?"

"Heavens, no! The mole people are creatures of the night. I would never have left our house after the sun went down. I even had trouble sleeping at night. I was always afraid they would sneak into my room and snatch me away."

My brother's face paled. "They do that?"

"There have been rumors but nothing was ever proven. The mole people only seem to care about food and not taking humans, thank goodness for that. But as a child, I had an active imagination, and I was sure they were going to come and get me in the night."

"Why don't they make their own food?"

I shook my head. Sometimes my brother asked the dumbest things. "They can't grow any food underground, stupid."

"Mom, Willie called me stupid," he whined.

"Now, Willie, you know better than that. Apologize

to your brother."

I grumbled an apology but I still thought he was dumb.

"He is right, Ed, the mole people cannot grow anything underground. It's even very difficult for us on the surface, since the wars, but fortunately we have valuable livestock."

"If they got hungry enough, I am sure they would eat humans," I added, just to bother my brother.

"Stop that, Willie. The mole people might not eat us but they are still dangerous, none the less. I am just glad they finally caught two of them. Maybe that will send a message to the others and keep them away from us."

A horn blasted from outside and my face lit up.

"There's your father. Now, run along and enjoy yourselves today. And for heaven's sake, don't get too close to that cage, or whatever they are holding those creatures in. You just look from a safe distance."

We had no time to answer Mother as Ed and I went out the side door in a flash and raced down to the car, climbing into the back seat.

Father smiled at us from the rearview mirror. "I would say you boys are a little excited, eh?"

We nodded our heads in unison.

"Well, get comfortable, the drive is going to be about an hour. The carnival is set up just outside the ruins of the Big City."

That news was almost as exciting as going to see the mole people. I had only ever seen the ruins of the Big City once in my life. It was an area that most folk generally avoided. It was inhabited now by undesirable types, and it was said that the mole people traveled more frequently through there, using old sewer and subway tunnels. The carnival would draw a lot of visitors so I would think that it would be safe for everyone to be there.

In school, I had seen photos of what the Big City looked like before the wars. It was marvelous. It was hard to imagine that buildings stood so tall at one time and so many people lived together in one place. The once grand city was now a cesspool for degenerates and outcasts.

My brother Ed was always the worrier.

"Is it safe to go near the Big City?" he asked.

"Don't worry, boys, there will be a lot of security at the carnival. This is probably the biggest attraction they've ever had."

"Dad, do you think the mole people look as weird as they do in our school books?" I wondered.

"They sure should. Enough folk have seen them before. You know, your Grandfather shot one of them once."

"Really? Gramps saw a mole person?"

"Yes, really. This was a long time ago, mind you, while I was still young. Gramps heard some sort of commotion outside one night, from the cows. His first thought was that perhaps a coyote was out there. He grabbed his shotgun and headed out toward the barn. That's when he came face to face with one of the mole people. The wretched creature carried a pitchfork but Gramps had his gun and shot the thing in the leg. It managed to escape but they never did come back to our barn again."

"Wow, Gramps never told us that story."

"It's a true story. I remember that shotgun blast woke the rest of us up that night. We all ran outside but all that was left was a blood trail through the field."

"What color was their blood?" Ed inquired.

"It was just red, same as ours."

We spent the rest of the drive in relative silence. My mind was swirling with excited thoughts of seeing the mole people. No doubt my stupid brother was having the same thoughts.

My excitement rose to an entirely new level when the carnival came into view. Giant flags and brightly-colored tents were spread across an open field, with the ruins of the Big City as an awe-inspiring backdrop. So focused was I on the carnival, that I barely even took note of the ruined skyscrapers in the distance.

It seemed as though a million vehicles were already here at the carnival and we were forced to park a fair distance from the entrance. The sun was particularly hot this day but even that could not bother me. My skin felt as though it was on fire by the time we bought our tickets and walked through the gates into the carnival.

I am sure my smile nearly swallowed my face. I glanced over to notice that Ed had the same goofy grin. We were instantly intoxicated by the heavenly smells around us. Vendors were selling everything from roasted corn to candied apples. The midway boasted a variety of different games and barkers shouted to all the kids, attempting to lure them in with dazzling prizes that could be easily won.

My Father didn't even have to ask us if we wished to play any games first. He knew our main concern was getting to the tent that housed the mole people and that tent was not difficult to locate. We just had to look for the largest gathering of people.

Ed, however, did get distracted by an ice cream stand and begged our father for an ice cream cone. He bought us each one and it didn't take my clumsy brother very long before some of his ice cream dripped onto my favorite green shirt.

"Dad, Ed spilled ice cream on my favorite shirt."

"Now, Ed, you be more careful."

"It's so hot out. The sun is melting my ice cream faster than I can lick it."

"Well, we will have some shade when we get inside that tent. Come along, boys, let's see what we came to see."

This was finally the moment. All the exuberant buildup had led to this. I knew we were in for something special by studying the faces of those who were leaving the tent. Expressions of joy and wonder were clearly etched on all the faces, young and old.

Our timing seemed to be impeccable. Even before we could maneuver our way through the thick crowd toward a large cage, a carnival barker announced that they were about to introduce the second mole person into the same enclosure. We could be in for a real treat now, I thought. Perhaps the mole people would fight each other. It was said the creatures could be quite vicious when provoked.

Everyone inside the tent was attempting to get the best spot to view the attraction. Fortunately, my father was able to clear a path through the crowd so that my brother and I had an unobstructed view. Both our jaws hung open in amazement. The two mole people looked as equally bizarre as the photos from my school books. They wore human clothes to appear like us but looked nothing like us.

The two strange creatures just stood motionless

223

within their cage, staring out at the gathered crowd. It didn't appear that they held any animosity toward each other and a fight between the two did not seem to be imminent. I wasn't too disappointed, however, just to see these rare things in the flesh was a still joy for me.

I wanted to get closer to the cage for a better look but feared getting any of my ice cream on the people around me.

"Dad, can you hold my ice cream?"

"Mine, too," Ed echoed.

"Oh, come on now boys, I only have four hands."

*　　*　　*　　*

The second man was shoved forcibly into the cage. He quickly noticed that he was not alone but did not recognize his fellow prisoner. His gaze shifted to the ghastly gathering of surface dwellers that were all staring back at him with clear amusement.

The first man turned to regard the other and saw clearly the look of horror upon his face. "This was your first trip to the surface, was it?"

"Yes," the second man answered.

"I have been up here many times but I never get used to seeing them. Who knew the surface radiation from the wars could produce such abominations all these years later?"

"Good heavens, look at the small one with the green shirt, holding the ice cream cones. It has two heads!"

THE CEMETERY KEEPER

Thunder cracked overhead and my eyes flew open. I hadn't yet fallen asleep but I felt I was close. It wasn't the storm that was keeping me up this night, it was the unbearable heat in my apartment. I had two fans running, with little success of cooling me off. All they seemed to do was circulate around the hot air.

Wiping sweat from my forehead, I rose from my bed to fetch a glass of water. My throat felt parched. I had little trouble navigating my way through my dark apartment with the aid of the constant lightning flashes from this horrendous storm. I reached my kitchen and fumbled about for a clean glass.

As I downed a mouthful of the refreshingly-cool water, I nearly choked from a sight that caught my eye outside the window. My apartment overlooked the creepy cemetery across the street. A strange light bobbed up and down within the shadows of the graveyard, giving me quite a start. I froze in place, momentarily wondering if I was observing the glow of some spirit from one of the thousands of dead residents.

I exhaled a sigh of relief when the outline of a person came into view, carrying a lantern. I watched as the person patrolled the interior side of the cemetery's gate. I continued to observe until the person, and the lantern, eventually vanished from sight behind one of the many buildings within the property.

I felt embarrassed for my moment of silliness, thinking that the newly-hired cemetery keeper was some undead creature that had risen from a grave. An unfortunate rash of vandalism had prompted the cemetery to hire an overnight keeper to keep the young punks away. A group of rotten young brats had recently found fun in tipping over headstones and spray painting on others. Despicable acts, if you ask me. I couldn't understand anyone's desire to walk through a graveyard at night, and disturb the resting places of the dead, no less.

So now the cemetery had some poor fellow patrol the property each night to ensure those rotten kids caused no further trouble. I felt bad for the man. I didn't envy him on the best of nights, but tonight in particular, was an awful night to have to patrol a cemetery. This storm would only amplify the creepiness of that place, tenfold. Just gazing upon the graveyard from my apartment window this night, was enough to raise goosebumps along my arms.

My financial predicament allowed for my current living arrangement. The only job I was able to land since moving to the Big City was stocking shelves in a department store. A minimum-wage salary didn't make living alone an easy task. I absolutely refused to live in the Junkie Jungle, the poorest neighborhood in the city, so this apartment was the next best option. When I first noticed the ad in the paper, I thought there was a typo with regards to the cost of the rent. It wasn't until I came to view the place that I understood why. There was reluctance in most people to live so close to a cemetery. Perhaps, it was some childhood fear that the dead would one day rise up to feast on the flesh of the living, or perhaps it was the daily reminder of what awaited us all in the end. One day we would all take up permanent residence within those gates for our eternal sleep.

For me, I believe, it was a little of both. I grew up on monster magazines and horror films at the picture show. I admit that even as an adult, I felt uneasy around graveyards. In the back of my mind, there was always that lingering thought of a hand reaching up from the ground to grab my ankle. Silly, I know, but unavoidable due to all the films I had watched where just such a thing had happened. And I did find it somewhat depressing to walk past that dreary place every day to go to and from work. It was a sad thought to think that I would slave away my life, working miserable jobs, only to end up buried in that cemetery with the rest of those unfortunate souls. That's what I had to look forward to.

But as I said, my finances dictated my decision to move into the apartment. I simply couldn't afford to live anywhere else. My apartment sat above a bakery in a two-story building, where all the apartments were situated above businesses. Far too many times, I was forced to purchase unneeded sweets, purely because of the aroma wafting through my windows. My waistline was also suffering as a result.

I would never be able to purchase a radio if those pastries kept dipping into my radio fund. With no radio, I passed away most evenings reading. And, at the sufferance of my imagination, all I had to read was my old monster magazines. Spooky stories and living next to a cemetery did not always make for a good combination. Horrible storms also did not help that equation. Thunder rumbled again and I made the decision to stop staring at the graveyard and get back into bed. I gave the cemetery keeper one last thought; pitying the man walking around out there in this storm, and then exhaustion set in and sleep claimed me.

Over the next week, the summer's heat attributed to more loss of sleep. I would toss and turn in my sweat-soaked sleepwear, until I was forced to the kitchen for a glass of water, or to place a wet towel onto my head. Each night, I took note of the poor cemetery keeper, making his rounds, ensuring the graveyard was free from vandalism. I had to wonder if this man was truly fearless, or was he simply that desperate for work? Often times, necessity drove people to do things that they would normally not. Personally, I could not imagine being desperate enough for money to patrol a graveyard at night. Not that I am belittling the work, or the good that that keeper is doing, but my mind would just not allow me to do it. So consumed would I be with childish thoughts of the undead, that I would most likely just flee in terror within the first half-hour. Clearly, this man did not harbor those same fears, or he found some way to successfully suppress them in order to collect a pay check.

Then I had to wonder, what one would be paid to

perform that duty? I surely hoped that man was getting paid more than the minimum wage that I was making. Granted, the act of patrolling the property was not a difficult one, but the mental stress afforded by the frightening surroundings alone, should be worth a pretty penny. But, knowing today's employers, I was certain he was not making nearly enough as he should be.

One Friday, I was asked to stay late at work to help with an inventory count of the entire department store. I readily agreed, since the overtime money would be quite helpful in boosting my radio fund. Every day at work, I had to listen to my fellow coworkers discussing the previous night's radio programs, but of course, I knew nothing of what they spoke of.

The sheer amount of inventory at the store made for a very long shift indeed. I was not walking home until very close to the midnight hour. The darkness had not bothered me overly much; that is until the cemetery came into view. I promptly crossed the street to avoid being so close to the surrounding wrought-iron gate. Very rarely was I ever out after dark. Looking at the cemetery from the safety of my apartment was one thing, walking past it at night was something entirely different.

Goosebumps ran down my arms and I quickened my pace. I felt slightly embarrassed, harboring childish thoughts that the monsters were going to get me. I nearly stumbled with fright, when a bobbing light caught the corner of my eye. I was relieved when I realized it was just the cemetery keeper making his rounds. I was able to slow down to a normal walking pace, as I now possessed a buffer. Surely the monsters would get him first, before me, due to his closer proximity.

I continued along, while keeping a subtle eye on the keeper. As he neared the gate, closest to the sidewalk on the opposite side of the street, he appeared to notice me and pause in his patrol. For a brief moment, curiosity nearly got the best of me, as the thought crossed my mind to speak with this man. Perhaps, I could get answers to the myriad amount of questions that filled my head. Even putting a name to this person would be welcomed. But, my baseless fear of the cemetery drove away any notion of engaging that man in any form of conversation during the night-time hours. I walked straight home and went to bed.

The next morning, I sat in the malt shop a block away from my apartment and sipped a coffee while reading the paper. One of the front page stories had caught my attention. Three teens had gone missing the previous night and have appeared to vanish without a trace. Friends said the three were on their way to the cemetery to cause mischief sometime around midnight. None of them returned home. Detective Kane was urging anyone that may have witnessed anything, to come forward with information.

I scratched my head in thought. Reports would have put those kids in or near the cemetery approximately around the time I was walking past to get home. I did observe the cemetery keeper patrolling last night. I would think that if those kids were up to no good, they would have been spotted by the keeper. That is why he was hired, after all. And yet the article made no mention of any employees having seen these potential trouble-makers. Could they have possibly eluded the man while he was making his rounds? Or, dark thoughts came to my mind, or could the keeper have something to do with their disappearance? While the idea of kids vandalizing graves was disgusting to me, I did not feel as though they should have gone missing because of it. Punished, yes, kidnapped or killed, no.

The thought that the cemetery keeper had something to do with this case nagged at me for several hours. As I looked out my window toward the graveyard, I decided I should go speak with the daytime manager. My first instinct was to call this Detective Kane, to relay my suspicions, but I determined that doing a little of my own detective work first was best, before jumping to conclusions.

*   *   *   *

I paced back and forth on the sidewalk in front of my building. It was getting close to midnight and I had yet to spot the cemetery keeper. After meeting with the cemetery manager earlier this afternoon, I had burning questions that required answers. My heart skipped a beat when suddenly the bobbing light from a lantern came into view.

I crossed the street immediately, making a straight line in the keeper's direction. I had uncovered some disturbing information and I felt that I was about to get to the bottom of this missing person's case. As the man neared the gate he appeared to notice my approach and I shouted.

"Hello? You there, hello? I need some answers from you."

The man remained silent and continued toward the gate with a slight stumble to his step. I bet he was drunk, I thought to myself.

"Just who are you?" I asked. "I spoke with the manager of the cemetery today and he told me they never hired anyone to patrol around here at night. He looked at me like I had three heads when I told him about watching you make your rounds each night."

The closer the man got, I nearly gagged from a god-awful stench. I managed to remain composed and continued with my questioning.

"I saw you here last night when those kids reportedly went missing. I am willing to bet that you saw them. I bet that you even know what happened to them."

The horrible smell intensified as the man reached the opposite side of the gate. He spoke not a word and reached for me through the iron bars with this free hand. I yelped and jumped back out of reach, to avoid being grabbed by a rotted hand. The light from the man's lantern illuminated his face and I quite nearly fainted from the mere sight of it. Like his hand, his face was rotted with his jaw bone clearly visible.

I am not above admitting that I screamed and ran for my life. The cemetery had never hired anyone to patrol at night. It would appear that the dead had unearthed their own keeper to take care of vandals.

THE WISHING WELL

Little Billy kicked a can through the field behind his house. Grasshoppers scattered in all directions at his approach. The afternoon sun had cooled off and made playing in the open field tolerable. Billy enjoyed spending time in the field and in the abandoned barn from the vacant lot nearby. He liked to pretend that the barn was a grand castle and that he was the king of said castle. Other times, he was a brave knight, dispatched from the castle to hunt down some marauding menace, like a fire-breathing dragon or a giant two-headed troll. He would find a suitable stick to substitute for his enchanted sword and slay the beasts to become the beloved hero of the realm.

Billy had very few friends, so he spent much of his time playing imaginary games alone. He and his mother lived in a ramshackle house on the far edges of town. The friends that he did have, lived too far away for him to visit. His mother did not own a car and they were too poor to afford a bicycle. When the school bus dropped Billy off at home in the afternoon, he would head out into the field and amuse himself. Today, however, he was not in the mood.

He continued to kick the can as if kicking it would solve his problems. Billy hated his math teacher. Mr. Dennis took great pleasure in terrorizing the kids and humiliating them whenever possible. He would laugh and call them stupid for answering questions incorrectly. In today's class, he pointed out the holes in Billy's shirt and told the rest of the students that Billy was an example of how not to dress. The only clean shirt Billy had available had holes in it. Mr. Dennis even inquired if Billy had been raised in a barn. The other kids laughed.

It was not the first time that Mr. Dennis had humiliated Billy in front of the others but the accumulation was beginning to take its toll. Billy dreaded going to math class and would feel sick to his stomach before entering the classroom. It was affecting his moods and he played less. Today, he just kicked the can about with his head down. He did not feel like slaying any dragons.

The can he had just kicked for the hundredth time, struck something solid, and the noise it made pulled Billy from his dark daydream. He looked around and realized that he was now on the far-western side of the abandoned barn. The side he never ventured to, as his own house and property was out of view. It always made Billy nervous if he couldn't see his property.

Curiosity defeated his nerves and he walked over to inspect an odd pile of tree branches. The can had struck something more solid than a branch and soon Billy was tossing them aside to reveal an old stone well, hidden beneath. He wondered why someone would have gone through the trouble of attempting to hide the well but then figured that perhaps it was for safety concerns. There were always stories of children falling into wells and Billy's own mother had warned him from time to time to be careful around them.

This particular well looked far older than any other well Billy had ever seen. There was something about the stones that it was built with. It stood nearly half as tall as the boy and the opening was roughly two feet across. Billy peered down the well but it was black as pitch and the bottom was out of sight. He found a small pebble and dropped it into the hole and was surprised that he never heard it land. No splash from water. No sound of stone on stone.

"Hello?" he shouted, and his voice echoed back at him five times.

Billy's stomach grumbled and he imagined that it would be close to dinner time. He stuck his hands in his pockets and turned back toward his house, kicking the can once again. His hand found the penny that he had hidden away in his left pocket. He generally kept his coins in his right pocket, a fact that was well known by Reggie, the school bully. Reggie had relinquished Billy of his nickel earlier that day, but Billy had stored a penny in the other pocket, allowing it to go unseen. He intended to buy a licorice stick with it, but after today's math class, he wasn't in the mood.

He paused for a moment to consider the words of his grandmother, who had said you could make a wish by tossing a coin into a well. She called them wishing wells. It was a difficult decision for Billy; make a silly wish or buy a licorice stick tomorrow. Under normal circumstances, Billy would never think to throw away a penny but these were desperate times. His mind was made when he considered that Reggie might just steal his penny tomorrow anyway. Better to throw it in the well than to hand it over freely to the bully.

Billy turned back to the well and leaned over. He spoke his wish aloud and tossed his only penny inside. It clinked once as it bounced off the side of the well but no sound of it landing was ever heard. He sighed and headed back home. He made it back just in time for dinner and to quiet his angry stomach.

The next day, Billy entered his math class accompanied by his usual feelings of anxiety. They awaited the arrival of Mr. Dennis, who was unusually late. As fifteen minutes went by, the class became restless. When twenty minutes had passed, Mr. Davidson, the principal, rushed into the classroom and informed them that Mr. Dennis was not in and proceeded to give the students some math problems to spend the rest of the class working on. Billy was obviously relieved to have a day without Mr. Dennis but it also made him curious about the timing of his absence. He pondered his wish, that Mr. Dennis would never bother him again, and then shook his head. It was just a silly wish. Wishes didn't really come true.

The following day, a substitute teacher was present in the math class when Billy arrived. He also noticed that police were inside the principal's office. The rumors around the school were that Mr. Dennis had just vanished. He was not at home and all attempts to find him had so far been unsuccessful. It was a complete mystery. Billy hated Mr. Dennis and did not feel sorry for him in the least, but his child's brain wondered, what would happen if anyone found out about his wish? Could he be held accountable for it? That was ridiculous, he thought, it was merely a coincidence.

A week passed by and still there was still no sign of Mr. Dennis. At lunch time on this particular day, Reggie was shaking down Billy for his lunch money, as per usual. This time, Billy had actually lost his nickel on the way to school. He had a newly found hole in his right pocket which must have attributed to the lost coin. Reggie, however, didn't believe the boy, and punched him hard in the stomach as a result. It took several moments before Billy could stand again and head for his next class.

After dinner that day, Billy begged his mother for a penny, which she reluctantly handed over, due to his skills of losing money. He then told her he wished to play outside before the sun disappeared and ran straight over to the old well. For quite some time, he just stood like a statue and stared at the well. Could it have really worked? he wondered. Or was it just a coincidence? Either way, he had decided to try it a second time.

Billy closed his eyes and spoke aloud. "I wish Reggie, the school bully, would disappear."

He tossed the coin into the well and again, heard nothing more. The sun was beginning to set behind a distant hill, so Billy ran home and spent most of the night awake, thinking about his wish.

When lunch time arrived the following day, Billy was shocked that Reggie was not waiting outside the back door of the school for him. He looked all over the schoolyard but the awful bully was nowhere in sight. Billy even decided to wait around, just to see if Reggie was running late, but the bully never showed up. The day passed with no Reggie and with no Mr. Dennis either.

Two days later, during dinner, Billy's mother noticed that her son was less talkative than usual.

"Something wrong, Billy?"

"No."

"Come on, you are even quieter than usual. Nothing you want to talk about?"

"Do wishes come true?"

"Wishes?"

"Yeah, like when you blow out the candles on your birthday cake and you are told to make a wish. Do those wishes ever come true?"

Billy's mother sat silent for a moment and considered the question. She figured her son was getting old enough now, that perhaps she shouldn't be telling him any more lies, and filling his head with fantasies. Life was not made up of fantasies and she supposed he should start getting used to that.

"Well no, Billy, those wishes don't come true. Believe me, if they did we wouldn't be living in this dump eating macaroni and cheese for dinner every night while your father lives in that mansion down the street, flaunting his wealth. That doesn't mean that the things you wish would come true, never will. You just have to make them happen on your own. There is no magical solution to make them come true."

"Oh."

"Why are you asking about wishes?"

"Well…"

"Yes?"

"Well, because I made two wishes and they came true."

"What wishes? What are you talking about?"

"I was playing over by the barn one day and I found this old well that someone had tried to hide."

"Now, Billy, you know you aren't supposed to wander away that far and you shouldn't be playing near any wells, they can be dangerous."

"I know but I was real careful. Anyway, I remember what Grandma said about wishing wells so I threw a penny in and made a wish."

"Is that why you asked me for a penny the other day? So you could throw it away into a well? You know we don't have a lot of money, Billy, you can't just go doing fool things like that."

"I know but Mr. Dennis was always so mean to me. Mean to everyone."

"Mr. Dennis? The missing teacher?"

"Yes. I wished that Mr. Dennis wouldn't bother me anymore and the next day he didn't show up to school. Nobody has seen him since I made that wish."

"Don't be so silly, that's just a coincidence."

"That's what I thought at first. So, I went back to the well and made another wish. This time I wished that Reggie the bully would disappear."

"Who is Reggie?"

"He is a bully. He takes my money every day at lunch time or punches me if he doesn't get it. I wished he would disappear and the next day he was gone. He also hasn't been seen since I made my wish."

Billy's mother tried to digest everything that she had just heard. It had to be a coincidence, wishes were not real.

She did her best to convince her son that those disappearances had nothing to do with his wishes and sent him along to his room to work on his homework.

Much later in the evening, when Billy had gone to bed, his mother threw on a sweater and went out the back door. The air was chill and the night was dark. The half-moon afforded little light, but once her eyes adjusted to the gloom, she set off in the direction of the barn.

Generations of her family had owned the land they lived on. After listening to Billy's story, she recalled a similar incident involving her parents. Her father had been a terrible drunk and physically abusive. Her mother used to say that she wished he would disappear one day, and then one day...he did. Billy's mother had always assumed that he just up and left. But, as Billy had reminded her, her mother used to tell them that if you threw a penny into a well and made a wish, that it would come true. She shook the nonsensical thoughts from her mind and marched toward the barn.

It took some effort to locate the well in the darkness but she eventually did. She stared at it for some time and wondered why there was a nervous feeling in her stomach. She thought to settle this silly notion of wishing wells and took a penny out of her wallet. She placed her wallet on the edge of the well and held the penny tightly, thinking of a stupid wish she could make. Her ex-husband was the first thought that came into her mind. Like her father had been, he was a drinker and a deadbeat. After abandoning her and Billy, he had come into some money and bought a large house just down the street. He never gave her a cent for Billy. She was positive that he only bought that house to torture her, as she had to pass it every single day on the way to work. Just the thought of him angered her so much. She was holding the penny so tightly, that it left an imprint on her palm. Her mind was made.

She closed her eyes and spoke her wish. "I wish my deadbeat ex down the road, Donny, would disappear."

She threw the penny into the well and waited to hear some kind of splash. There was nothing. She waited for...something...she wasn't sure what. She thought maybe there would be some kind of feeling that the wish worked. Perhaps, some kind of tingling sensation. When she felt nothing at all, she turned and walked back toward her house. She scolded herself for even coming out here and wasting a perfectly good penny. Earlier, she had been telling her son not to be foolish and believe in wishes, and then she had come out to the well and did the very same thing.

About half-way back, Billy's mother realized she had forgotten her wallet at the well. She cursed to herself and turned back. As she approached the well, movement caught her attention and froze her place. She was unsure if the darkness was playing tricks with her eyes but she stood motionless, nonetheless. Something crawled its way out of the well. Something dark and something vaguely humanoid. A horrendous stench suddenly assaulted her nostrils and she fought back the urge to vomit. It was the unmistakable stench of decay. Whatever that thing was, it smelled as if it had been dead for a very long time.

Its movements were jerky and sent shivers all over her body. She stifled a scream as it sniffed at the air, as though it detected her presence. She exhaled as it stood unsteadily, on two legs, and then shambled off away from her; off in the direction of Donny's house.

MONSTERS IN THE CLOSET

Mrs. Brookfield entered the office wearing a mask of concern. Behind her, she pulled her ten-year-old.

"Dr. Phinn, it has started again. Little Norbert thinks the monster is back in his closet. He hasn't slept in two days."

"I don't think it is there, I know it is there," her son responded.

Mrs. Brookfield shook her head in frustration. "You see? Whatever are we to do? I thought he was over this? He was doing so well."

"Alright, give Norbert and me some time to talk."

Mrs. Brookfield left the office muttering under her breath. "You think you have done everything right. Raised all our children the same way. You would think they would understand that there is no such thing as monsters. I mean really, monsters? Just ridiculous."

"Have a seat, Norbert," Dr. Phinn suggested, once his mother had closed the door behind her. "How have you been?"

"Okay."

"Just, okay?"

"Yeah."

"It doesn't sound like everything is okay. What's this about the monster coming back to your closet? I thought it left months ago?"

"It did."

"And you are certain it is back again? You are sure that maybe you just didn't imagine it this time, or maybe it was just a nightmare you had?"

"No. I heard it in my closet and then it even opened the door to peek at me."

Dr. Phinn opened a file folder on his desk and pulled out a sketch of Norbert's monster. "So, did it look exactly the same? A shadow creature with horns and wings and dull, red-colored eyes?"

Norbert fidgeted nervously with the buttons on this shirt. "Yes."

"So, now you are losing sleep again? You are worried it is going to get you?"

"Yes."

"I imagine you had your parents check the closet again? They didn't find anything, did they?"

"No. It leaves before they come."

Dr. Phinn nodded and wrote a few things down in a notebook. "These monsters are clever, aren't they?"

Norbert shook his head in agreement.

"So, when you left your lamp on at night, that seemed to work? Correct?"

"Uh huh."

"Yes, you see these shadow creatures fear the light. Even something as faint as a bedside lamp is enough to hurt their sensitive eyes. I am going to suggest leaving the lamp on again each night. I believe the creature will become frustrated eventually and leave for good."

"You still believe me?"

"Of course I do. You are not my only patient with monsters in their closet. It is actually a more common thing than folk want to believe."

"Why don't my parents ever believe me?"

"Well, there are some people who have never seen one of these monsters before, so for them it is hard to imagine that they exist. Then there are others who have seen them before but do not wish to acknowledge their existence anymore. It brings back frightening memories of when they were a child and they just want to forget about them and pretend it never happened."

"Have you seen them before, Dr. Phinn?"

"I will tell you something in confidence, Norbert, because we are friends. Yes, I have seen these shadow monsters before."

"Really? In your closet?"

"Yes, when I was about your age, one of them chose to visit my closet quite regularly. I can remember feeling very scared that it would get me and I lost a lot of sleep as well."

"What did you do?"

"As you can see, I am still here. It never got me. I left two lamps on at night for almost three months and the monster, I assume, grew too restless waiting for me to turn the lights off again and decided to leave me alone. It never returned to my closet ever again."

"My parents don't like it when I keep my lamp on. It disturbs my father's sleep and they say it is more expensive."

"You let me speak to your mother about that. Now, how about you go out there and tell her to come back in for a moment. And just remember, Norbert, the lamp will keep the monster away. I am positive that it will not be able to get you."

Norbert nodded and went into the waiting room to inform his mother that Dr. Phinn wished to speak with her. She returned to the office and closed the door behind her. Despite being offered a seat, the woman elected to pace about the room.

"Well? What are we to do? He is positive there is a monster in his closet and he simply cannot sleep because of it."

"I have advised him to just leave his lamp on for a while longer. That seemed to help before."

"That is easy for you to suggest, you don't pay our electricity bill. And my husband has trouble sleeping with that light coming from right across the hall."

"Mrs. Brookfield, I have told Norbert that the light from his lamp will keep the monster away. Allow him to leave it on for a while longer and soon he will forget about the monster."

"I admit I am no expert on such things but shouldn't you be trying to explain to him that there is no such thing as monsters? You tell him that the lamp will keep the monster away, so you are confirming that there is a monster."

"Can you not recall being that young? A child's mind works differently from ours. They still cannot differentiate between fantasy and reality. Norbert truly believes that there is a monster in his closet and you cannot convince him otherwise. The best thing to do is to play along and suggest things that will chase away the monster. He will be reluctant to share his concerns with you if you are always telling him that he is lying or imagining things. Norbert isn't the only child I deal with that believe monsters live in their closet. It is a common belief for children. They are either in the closet or hiding under the bed, just waiting for those lights to go off. Trust me, Mrs. Brookfield, I have much experience with this stuff."

"Oh I know, I have done my research. You are considered one of the best child psychologists in the Big City. Your fees can attest to that."

Dr. Phinn chuckled. "Believe it or not, I am trying to prevent you from having to come back here. Norbert is an otherwise very normal child. Just allow him to keep the lamp on and his problems will go away. As he gets older, he will forget about monsters and these worries will disappear. I see it all the time."

"We will see, I suppose. Well, thank you for your time again, Dr. Phinn."

"It is my pleasure."

The following week, another concerned parent brought their nine-year-old child to Dr. Phinn's office. Sammy had apparently gotten very little sleep for over a month, due to a monster in his closet. It was beginning to affect him at school as he would frequently doze off in class.

Dr. Phinn sat in his chair with a fresh new notebook, while Sammy sat on the sofa nearby.

"So, Sammy, your mother tells me you believe there is a monster in your closet?"

"Yes, sir."

"Do you just hear it, or have you also seen it, by chance?"

"Both, kinda. Sometimes I can hear it scratching around in there. Like it scrapes its claws on the back of the door. Sometimes, if I forget to close the door all the way, I can see it peeking out at me."

Dr. Phinn made notes while Sammy spoke. "And when it peeks at you, what do you do?"

"Um, well like sometimes I will run into my parent's room and like well other times I just hide under the blankets."

"And when you hide under the blankets, it goes away?"

"Usually, cuz then it can't see me."

"Yes, I have heard these monsters possess limited intelligence. They can be easily fooled by blankets."

"You know about these monsters? My parents say I am making it up. They say it is all because my older brother took me to the picture show to see a scary film."

"Oh, I see. What film was it?"

"The Creeping Thing."

"I wasn't aware they allowed children your age to see films like that."

"Well, um, my brother kinda snuck me in a back door."

"Ah. Did the film scare you?"

"Yes."

"And how long after that, would you say, that you started hearing the monster in your closet?"

"Um, a few days later."

"I see."

"I am not making it up. I saw it."

"Oh, I am sure you are not making it up. I can just understand why your parents might think it is related to the film you saw. But to answer your earlier question, yes, I do know a bit about these monsters. I believe you are telling the truth."

Sammy paled, slightly. "So, it is real?"

"I am afraid, so, yes. But these monsters are just curious creatures, and as you have already experienced, easily fooled. Have you ever wondered why it has never come out of your closet and, well, got you?"

"Cuz I am good at hiding."

"Well, that is part of it, yes. These monsters just like to observe humans and try to learn from us. They are content with only watching from the closet where they think that nobody can see them. Once you hide under the blankets, it believes you have disappeared, and then it will grow bored and simply leave."

"But even after I do that, it comes back again."

"Every night?"

"No. Every couple days."

"So, you have seen it a few times? Can you describe it to me?"

Dr. Phinn began sketching in his notebook as Sammy described the monster. "Um, it's like all black, like a shadow. Um, it has horns and wings."

"Wings like a bird?"

"Um, no. Wings like a bat."

"And its eyes? Can you remember?"

"Its eyes are red."

"Bright red?"

"Um, no. More dull."

Dr. Phinn completed a sketch that looked very similar to Norbert's monster. It resembled the monster of several other of his patients as well.

"Yes, these shadow monsters are quite common. And quite harmless, I can assure you."

"How come my parents can never see it? Even my big brother makes fun of me. He can't see it either."

"These monsters are afraid of anything larger than they are. They avoid adults and older children."

"How can I get rid of it?"

"Just keep doing what you are doing. Stay under the blankets where it cannot see you and eventually, as I said, it will grow bored and leave. It will find someone else's closet to visit."

"It won't get me?"

"No, it won't get you. It will not even know you are there if you remain out of sight under the covers."

Sammy's parents had to return two other times, as their son, while still hiding under the blankets, claimed he could still hear the monster scratching the closet door. The monster apparently left after Dr. Phinn thought to give Sammy a "magical" necklace that was created to ward off monsters. In truth, it cost a penny and came out of a vending machine.

Norbert's parents also brought him back several months later, quite frustrated. Dr. Phinn suggested using the necklace, and so far, to his parent's delight, Norbert's monster had disappeared.

One evening, Dr. Phinn stayed late at his office in order to organize some files. His office was located on the second floor of a building which housed various other offices. Dr. Phinn noticed the time and was running late for an appointment. He stepped out of his office and into the hallway, but before he could lock the door, a voice gave him a start.

"You are Dr. Phinn?"

The man appeared to be in his forties and glanced about nervously, with bloodshot eyes. If Dr. Phinn had to guess, he would say that the man had not slept for days.

"Yes, I am. What can I do for you, sir? I am running late for an appointment, elsewhere."

"My name is Franklyn Wade and I was told that you might be able to help me with a problem I am having. I have not been able to sleep as of late."

"Well, Mr. Wade, I am child psychologist. I do not have any adult clients."

"I figured that but I was told you are familiar with my problem."

"And what problem might that be?"

"I know how crazy this might sound but I believe I have a monster in my closet."

"I see."

"An employee of mine said that she brought her son here to speak with you about a monster. She told me that you were able to solve her problem and to make the monster go away."

"Well, as I said, I don't have any adult clients but if you wish to call in the morning and book an appointment, we could possibly have a chat."

"I can't wait until the morning. I haven't been able to sleep at all. Can we not just talk now?"

"It is after hours, Mr. Wade, and I have an appointment to get to."

"Please, I beg you! I am quite wealthy, I will pay double whatever you would normally charge for a session."

"Being after hours, my fee would already be double what it would be in the morning."

"I don't care. I will pay you double that, then. Please, can we just go inside and talk?"

"Very well, come inside."

Dr. Phinn turned all the lights back on and directed the man to have a seat on the sofa in his office. The money was definitely a contributing factor to his decision to entertain this individual, but truth be told, the doctor was a little intrigued to hear his tale. He picked up a fresh notebook and indicated to Mr. Wade that he may begin.

"You probably think I am nuts."

"No, Mr. Wade, I do not."

"I know what you must be thinking, though. You are thinking, what is an adult doing here complaining about a monster in his closet? That is the stuff of a child's imagination."

"I wasn't thinking that at all."

"Have you ever heard an adult say there is a monster in their closet?"

"Well, no, but there is always a first for everything. And as I said, I deal strictly with children. Tell me, Mr. Wade, have you been to the picture show lately? Have you watched any scary films?"

"Oh, I know where this is going. You think I am suffering from some kind of nightmare due to watching a horror film. I assure you, doctor, I do not frighten so easily. And no, I have not been to the picture show to see anything in quite some time."

"It was merely a simple question. I wasn't implying anything. Let's get right to the monster then, shall we? How do you know there is one in your closet? Have you seen it?"

"I have. I wouldn't be sitting here talking to you if I thought I was imagining the whole thing."

"Tell me about it."

"It started a few weeks ago. At first there was scratching sounds from inside the closet. My first thought was mice. So I would ignore it at first and then just look in the morning, but I could find no traces of mice."

"Did anyone else in the household hear these noises?"

"No, I live alone."

"So, when did you first see it?"

"I would say it was the fourth night of hearing noises when I finally got out of bed and opened the closet door," Mr. Wade visibly shuddered as he recalled that night. "It was standing right there in my closet. Right there staring me in the face."

"What was? Describe what you saw."

Mr. Wade stood up from the sofa and began pacing about. "You won't believe this."

"Try me."

"It was more of a shape in the darkness. Like a shadow. It felt as though if I reached out for it my hand would pass straight through."

"What did the shape look like?"

"It stood about as tall as me and was jet black. I could make out small horns and large wings."

"What about its eyes? Could you see any eyes?"

"Yes, they were yellowish. A kind of sickly yellow."

Dr. Phinn paused during his sketch of the monster and looked up. "Yellow eyes, you say?"

"Yes, yellow eyes. I can admit I yelled in fright and slammed the closet door shut. I ran downstairs and spent the rest of the night sitting on my sofa. I know what I saw. It was real, doctor. I know I am a grown man but there was no way I imagined what I saw. I was not dreaming. I was wide awake."

"No, no, I believe you, Mr. Wade."

"What can I do about this? Nobody else will believe me?"

Dr. Phinn scratched his head. "Well, there is a magical necklace, but it is not cheap."

The doctor explained the necklace and its success rate with warding off the monsters. Desperate, the man paid for the necklace and the session before leaving.

Dr. Phinn locked the door behind the man and then returned to his desk.

"Yellow eyes," he kept repeating to himself, as he flipped through the pages of his personal phone book. "Yellow eyes."

He found the number he sought and picked up his phone and dialed. It was late, he knew, but the detail of the yellow eyes bothered him. He needed answers.

"Hello? Dr. Ryanne?"

Pause.

"This is Dr. Phinn. I apologize for the lateness of this call but something has come up tonight."

Pause.

"Yes, well, I just had a client leave my office moments ago. He claims to have seen a monster in his closet with yellow eyes. Yellow eyes, Dr. Ryanne. And the client was an adult male. An adult. I thought we agreed to leave adults alone? We are only to frighten the children."

Pause.

"I don't care if you needed the extra money. The man came here to see me anyway, not you. We have built ourselves a remarkable business here by only scaring the children. Adults will only cause us headaches, believe me, Dr. Ryanne."

Pause.

"Well, I sold this man one of those ridiculous necklaces so just stay away from his house at ninety-one Wellsprings."

Pause.

"That's fine but let's just be smart about this in the future. I don't want to jeopardize what we have going here. We have the child come in for a few sessions, then cure them and stop visiting their closets. We need those word-of-mouth referrals that our therapy sessions actually work."

Pause.

"Alright, good. Now, I must be off. I am running extremely late. I was supposed to be in someone's closet hours ago. I hope they have not yet fallen asleep."

Pause.

"Yes, good night to you, Dr. Ryanne."

Dr. Phinn hung up the phone, shaking his head. He

removed his jacket and tie and placed them carefully on his chair, so as not to wrinkle them. His body began to shake and shudder until he transformed back into his natural form. A form that was more shadow than substance. The creature with the dull red eyes flew out of the office window, carried by bat-like wings, toward his appointed closet.

ABOUT THE AUTHOR

Jeremy was born in Scarborough, Ontario, Canada. He started creating his own characters and writing his own stories by the age of 9. He is a boxing fanatic, having been an amateur boxer and is now a professional boxing judge. In his spare time when not watching boxing, or reruns of Lost in Space and Rocket Robin Hood, Jeremy tries to find time to write some of the many stories floating around in his head.

41390452R00156

Made in the USA
Middletown, DE
07 April 2019